PENGUIN METRO READS

LITTLE THINGS

Dipen Shah was born in Mumbai and spent most of his childhood in Doha, Qatar. He started working as a copywriter after completing his bachelor's in media and communications. Later, he wrote content for Indian Premier League (IPL) teams like Royal Challengers Bangalore and Kings XI Punjab before moving to FilterCopy, Dice Media and Gobble as a social media manager. Currently, he is a copy editor at FilterCopy. Dipen loves comedy and hopes to become a comedian someday. He is also a hopeless romantic. He lives in Mumbai.

Dice Media is the web series division of Pocket Aces Pictures Pvt. Ltd.

A DICE MEDIA ORIGINAL SERIES

LITTLE THINGS

Based on a screenplay by Dhruv Sehgal

DIPEN SHAH

Penguin
metro reads

An imprint of Penguin Random House

PENGUIN METRO READS

USA | Canada | UK | Ireland | Australia
New Zealand | India | South Africa | China | Singapore

Penguin Metro Reads is part of the Penguin Random House group of companies
whose addresses can be found at global.penguinrandomhouse.com

Published by Penguin Random House India Pvt. Ltd
4th Floor, Capital Tower 1, MG Road,
Gurugram 122 002, Haryana, India

Penguin
Random House
India

First published in Penguin Metro Reads by Penguin Random House India 2018

ISBN 9780143441519

Typeset in Aldine401 BT by Manipal Digital Systems, Manipal
Printed at Repro India Limited

CONTENTS

FOMO

1

'What do you think?' Kavya asked as she turned away from the bedroom mirror and faced Dhruv.

Dhruv looked up from his laptop and was awestruck. He was sitting in his nightclothes on the bed and working. She looked so adorable! The pink saree matched her rosy lips perfectly, and she was also wearing an ornate nose ring.

'Wow!' he finally managed to say, continuing to stare at her.

He wondered how he had managed to woo Kavya. She was a head-turner with a fair complexion, slim figure and a mop of dense curls, while he was dark, of average height and build, nothing to write home about. She loved people, was always up for socializing and never failed to make friends, but you could not say the same about him. He was a food connoisseur and preferred to stay at home, reading and watching football.

Dhruv picked up his mobile phone to take a picture of Kavya. She protested, complaining that she didn't think she looked her best, but struck a pose anyway when he didn't lower the phone.

So damn cute, Dhruv said to himself as he uploaded her picture on Snapchat. He tried to think of something romantic to say, something poetic that would truly express the burst of love he was feeling for her. But as was often the case, the words didn't come to him.

He simply said, 'You look so beautiful, Kavvu!'

Kavya didn't seem to hear him as she continued to examine herself in the mirror. She was trying to decide what to wear for her friend Prachi's wedding the following month. She needed to look perfect. She had even found the perfect nose ring, or so she thought.

All she needed now was the perfect saree to go with it.

'When did you buy that nose thingy?' Dhruv asked.

'It's called a *nath*, Dhruv! It's a Maharashtrian design. Remember I told you I was saving up for it? I bought it a couple of weeks back.'

And then, before he could stop himself, Dhruv blurted out, 'Something like that would make anyone look pretty, wouldn't it?

Sometimes when you're dumbstruck, you end up saying dumb things.

'Thanks, Dhruv! How charming!' Kavya was a little miffed. She continued scrutinizing herself and then added, 'Anyway, I don't think the nath goes with this saree. And this saree is also not very shaadi-types. I think I'm going to try on something new.'

This still wasn't over? Dhruv was horrified. It was so late at night! Was it going to take more time? Couldn't Kavya's dress rehearsal continue the next day?

Dhruv was worried about the next morning. They had planned to leave early for corn bhajis. He had been waiting for weeks to sink his teeth into them. Images of the bhajis popped up in his mind, and he could almost smell them!

'Kavvu, please hurry up! We have to leave at 4 a.m. if we have to reach there before the shop opens at 6.30 a.m. I've checked—the woman who sells the bhajis only sits for two hours.'

'Yeah, yeah, just give me two minutes,' Kavya called out from the bathroom.

By the time Kavya returned, now wearing a different saree, Dhruv had put his laptop away and was reading a book. She asked him again how it looked. All he said was 'nice', sounding disinterested.

Not convinced, she tried on a few more sarees, but Dhruv's responses were the same, just sleepier with every passing minute, till he finally said 'it's nice' without even looking at her.

'Dhruv, stop saying "it's nice" to everything! Say something different!' Kavya was exasperated.

Groggy and annoyed by now, Dhruv replied, 'But it is just nice, not amazing! It's too late, yaar. My mind is not working. Kavvu, just come to bed, please. We have to get up at 4 a.m. and travel two hours. I really want to eat those bhajis!'

Kavya made a face, hell-bent on selecting the right saree before going to sleep. Dhruv's response irritated her even more. 'None of these sarees are amazing, and they don't even go well with the nath! I'm so annoyed. I think I'll have to just go and buy something new for Prachi's wedding,' she mused, and then catching Dhruv's annoyed expression added hurriedly, 'Okay, I'll come in two minutes, you sleep.'

'Good night!' Dhruv was relieved.

'Good night.'

* * *

It wasn't the chirping of birds that Kavya woke up to—it was the sound of traffic. She looked at her mobile phone and checked the time.

Oh God! Dhruv was going to be pissed. She didn't have the heart to wake him up just yet or the energy to deal with the yelling that would follow. She decided to go through her friends' Snapchat stories instead. Suddenly, Kavya felt jealous looking at pictures of their happening lives.

She consoled herself with the thought that what she had with Dhruv was above everything else. *He looks so cute while sleeping*, she thought before clicking a selfie and putting it up as her Snapchat story with the caption 'Sleeping in! #LazySunday'.

Feeling more prepared for the storm that seemed inevitable, Kavya gently shook Dhruv to wake him up. 'Wake up, Momo!' she whispered. It was a nickname she used when she felt particularly affectionate towards him. If there was any time that she needed to use this, it was now. On getting no reaction from him, she shook him more vigorously. 'Wake up!'

'Let me sleep for two more minutes,' said a groggy Dhruv.

'It's 12.30 p.m., Dhruv,' Kavya said softly.

'What!' Dhruv sat up bolt upright. 'Shit! We missed it!' He smacked his forehead with his palm.

'Did you forget to set the alarm?' inquired Kavya.

'I must have.'

Then he turned to her. 'Because of your whole saree thing!'

'Hey, how is this my fault? Don't turn this around on me, Dhruv. You forgot to set the alarm!'

'Yeah! Because I was sleepy and confused. *Arre* yaar, I really wanted to eat those bhajis today!'

Kavya looked at him and did not say anything. She felt he would be all right if she left him alone for a while.

2

Twenty minutes later . . .

A visibly upset Dhruv still couldn't believe that he had again missed out on the bhajis he so desperately wanted to eat.

Even Kavya felt sorry for him and tried to console him. 'What's the point of brooding? We've lost half the day anyway.'

Then, because she didn't want to ruin a Sunday, especially after seeing pictures on Snapchat of her friends having so much fun, she added, 'Others are having such a good time. And we're sitting here in bed and—'

'Yeah, we were supposed to have a great time too.'

'Yeah, but what is the point of us fighting now?' Kavya asked in a placatory tone. But that did nothing to console him. She thought fast, and an idea came to her. It was damage-control time.

'I know how to turn this Sunday around. Give me thirty minutes and I'll fix something for you.'

She gave Dhruv a peck on the cheek, something that never failed to brighten his day, and jumped out of bed. There was a lot to be done. Dhruv picked up his mobile phone and saw something on Snapchat that annoyed him further. His friend Akash was having a blast in Goa.

He remembered the time he had dragged Kavya to Goa for a long weekend. She had never been there and hadn't been very interested or excited about it either. But once they were there, neither of them had wanted to come back. It was their first vacation together, something that had brought them closer. *God! I wish I could relive those three days, they really were the best days of my life*, Dhruv thought. But that was long ago—many responsibilities and many disappointments ago—before he had to worry about EMIs, mutual funds and research grants, even before Kavya had moved in with him. So much had changed since then—some good, some not so good. However, one thing that remained constant was the unrelenting, never-faltering love and support that Kavya showered on him. He was extremely grateful for that.

The clanking of utensils from the kitchen brought Dhruv spiralling back to reality. And the reality was that he was extremely jealous of Akash.

'*Kutta*,' Dhruv mumbled, still hurting from the disappointing start to the Sunday.

Now that his bhaji plan had failed, he desperately tried to focus on redeeming whatever was left of the day. He was scrolling through social media when he found what looked like an amazing place for Keralite cuisine. His heart started pounding again. The prospect of trying out new, good food was something that always got him excited—perhaps even more than sex or Liverpool winning a championship. His mind, now diverted from the bhajis, had something new to look forward to. He rushed to tell Kavya about it. He burst into the dining room. 'Kavvu, we have to check out this new Kerala place. It looks kick-ass!'

Even as he spoke, he noticed the sumptuous spread on the table: waffles with maple syrup, fresh orange juice, fried mushrooms, bacon strips, sliced fruits, eggs, toast and other things he couldn't even name. Kavya had gone all out to prepare a brunch that would make up for them missing out on the bhajis. She stood there, beaming at him.

He was grateful. Yes, he was. But as usual, stupid things tended to escape from his mouth without him even realizing it. 'It's not possible to go there now, is it?'

Kavya's smile vanished. 'At least appreciate the effort, Dhruv!'

Realizing his mistake and fully aware of how things could head south in no time, Dhruv immediately tried to calm her.

'Hey, I obviously appreciate all the effort you put into this. Thank you so much! It's just that I got carried away. Bombay Bhukkad put up this new post and I thought that it would be nice to try something new today.'

It worked. Kavya knew his weakness for food, and anyway she couldn't stay mad at him for long.

As she whipped out her mobile phone to capture the feast spread out on the table, Dhruv swooped down on the juice.

'One minute, one minute!' Kavya called out. She had made them a brunch worthy of kings, and she wasn't going to let this opportunity to show off on Snapchat pass by.

Dhruv wasn't much into capturing every moment on social media. In fact, he thought it was silly. But who was he to take away this joy from Kavya after she had worked so hard for it? So, he kept quiet, made a goofy face, gargled with the juice in his mouth and posed playfully.

This'll show them! Kavya thought as she posted the photo. She knew it was silly, but she was experiencing some serious FOMO (Fear of Missing Out) with all their friends travelling over the weekend.

'Baconnnnn!' sang Dhruv, picking up a strip. He was about to bite into it when Kavya stopped him.

'What? Please let me eat, I'm hungry. Please!'

Kavya broke into a giggle. 'Just get the mustard sauce first, please?'

Dhruv got up from his chair with a smile and nudged Kavya playfully. 'It's such an amazing experience, dude.'

'What?'

'To date a sloth bear like you!'

'I'm not lazy, okay? I'm just chilled out!' Kavya struck a meditation pose.

14

'Of course, of course! That is exactly the case. You're right, definitely right.' Dhruv mocked her.

'But I made all this!'

'I know, I know. I am just joking!' Dhruv went halfway, came back and said, 'It all looks so great, and I mean it. Thank you!' He bent down to kiss her.

She cheered up immediately. *It's amazing how he can make me feel like this even after all this time*, Kavya thought, every fibre of her being singing with happiness.

Post-brunch, Kavya was lazing around on the couch in the hall with her laptop when Dhruv walked in, swinging his mobile phone from side to side, looking for another Pokémon on Pokémon Go. In the process, he bumped into a plant and a sofa and almost fell over, but continued undeterred on his quest. Finally, he said with disappointment, 'How come I can't find any Pokémons in our house? Viraj found two, you know?'

Kavya looked up. Dhruv was standing in front of her with an exasperated look on his

15

face. On the wall to his right was a huge poster of Liverpool, his favourite football club, and behind him was a comic strip from *Calvin and Hobbes* which both of them adored. The wall to his left was covered with posters of movies, TV shows, bands, artists and albums that they loved.

Kavya had problems of her own. Right now, the pictures of her friends on social media having fun were making her feel low while she spent her Sunday at home.

'Dude, this Megha keeps travelling all the time! It's not fair! She even went to a Coldplay concert. Look.'

Dhruv came over to take a look. 'Cool, man!' he exclaimed, and then went back to his game, once again brandishing his mobile phone all over the room.

'Okay! Listen, let's watch a film,' Kavya suggested, still determined to have a fun Sunday.

'Oh! Isn't it my turn?' Dhruv glanced slyly at Kavya to see if she remembered.

'No, it's mine!' she said with a smile, knowing fully well that he was trying to trick her.

'Shit! You remembered!' he was a tad disappointed.

They had a pact. Every time they watched a movie together, they took turns to decide what to see. 'Three, two, one . . .' Dhruv started the countdown.

Kavya had to decide quickly.

'*Inside Out!*'

'No! No, no, no, no . . .' Dhruv wailed. He left his search for Pokémons and sat next to Kavya.

'Hey, what's your problem? I've heard it's a good film.'

'Yeah, it's a very good film. But the problem is that it is an animated film. And all these films have at least two or three moments that make you cry. Then you'll get sentimental and stop talking. I'll keep asking you, "Kavvu, what happened?" but you won't reply or talk. But then, at exactly 7 p.m., you'll want to talk.

17

And that is the time Liverpool will be playing Chelsea . . .'

Kavya made a face.

'. . . And then you'll make a face. Exactly this face! Hold that expression!' said Dhruv, holding up his hands as if framing her face. 'So pretty when pissed off!'

3

They were watching *Inside Out*. Kavya lay with her head on Dhruv's lap, completely immersed in the movie as Happy and Bing Bong tried to sing their way out of the abyss of forgotten memories, when she heard some sniffles.

She looked up to see Dhruv biting his lip, about to cry. *How the tables had turned!*

'Are you okay?' Kavya had a naughty smile playing on her face.

'Yeah, obviously.' Dhruv's voice was quavering slightly.

'Are you sure?'

'Yes!' he exclaimed, pretending like nothing had happened.

Kavya paused the movie, sat up and pulled Dhruv's cheeks.

'Oh, so cute! You cried and all!'

'This is why I did not want to watch this movie. Akash is having a ball in Goa, chilling on the beach with beer. And look at me. I'm sitting here mourning Bing Bong.'

'Hey! Don't ruin it like that! It's a good movie.'

'Yeah, I know it is good. But I just wanted to watch something relaxed and funny.'

With Dhruv so emotionally charged, Kavya knew enjoying the movie would be a task.

'Hey, you want to go to the arcade and play air hockey with me instead? It's been a while since I kicked your ass at it anyway.'

Kavya smirked, and Dhruv frowned.

'No way! Liverpool plays Chelsea at 7 p.m., and there's no way I am missing that!' Dhruv was firm.

Kavya was in no mood to sit at home, so she teased him some more. 'So what? Just one game. Come on! Don't tell me you're chicken!'

'Okay, fine. One game and we'll come back by 7 p.m. Okay?'

'Sure, you're on!'

* * *

'You know, you shouldn't wear kajal on Sundays,' Dhruv told Kavya as they made their way to the gaming arcade at the mall.

'The way you don't shower on Sundays?' Kavya pinched her nose. She had bathed, changed and even put on some make-up. Dhruv, on the other hand, looked as if he had just got out of bed.

'Exactly! At least once a week we should know what we really look like without make-up and fancy clothes. I think it's quite intense. It's very naked, no? Being exactly who you are?'

Kavya refused to take the bait. She had lost interest already. Dhruv would keep getting into these long-winded, intense discussions about things that seemed inconsequential to her. Fortunately, she didn't have to keep listening any more. They had reached the mall.

Dhruv stepped inside while Kavya got her bag checked at the security counter. Almost immediately, Dhruv was approached by a middle-aged man dressed formally, the mall's security ID around his neck. As Kavya caught up, the man began to question Dhruv.

'Excuse me, Sir. If you don't mind me asking, where are you going?'

'To play games.'

Kavya corrected him. 'The arcade, Dhruv, it's called an arcade.' Dhruv wanted to tease Kavya about how sophisticated she pretended to be whenever she went out when he was interrupted.

'You can't go in, Sir,' the man declared.

Annoyed, Dhruv asked, 'Why? What's the scene? Who the hell are you?'

'Sir, I'm the manager of this mall. I'm sorry but I can't let you go upstairs. You see, there's a child's birthday party going on in the arcade. And you have "In Cock We Trust" written on your T-shirt.'

Dhruv glanced at his clothes. He was wearing his favourite Sriracha sauce T-shirt—a hot sauce and a piece of clothing he held very dear. The logo of this sauce was a rooster, which is why the caption 'In Cock We Trust'.

'Yeah, so?' Dhruv didn't get the point.

'Sir, someone might file a complaint. It could become an issue. Please try and understand.' Worry was evident on the manager's face and in his voice.

'This is my favourite chilli sauce brand's T-shirt.'

'Sriracha is the name of a sauce, Sir,' Kavya said.

But their explanations and arguments were to no avail.

'Ma'am, that doesn't matter. If even one person complains, it can become an issue. Please try and understand. Plus, today is my first day at work. Please don't put my job at risk. Please.'

'Don't talk rubbish, man! We want to play a few games. Just let us in.' Dhruv was losing patience.

However, the manager remained adamant.

'Sir, please try and understand. Someone could file a complaint. This could put my job at risk.' He was almost blocking their way by now.

Seeing the man's earnestness, Kavya gave in. She caught Dhruv's eye and nudged him along, signalling that it was best they left. As a final act of defiance, Dhruv shouted, 'How can you do this, yaar? This is unacceptable!' He then turned to follow Kavya, who was already on her way out.

As Kavya and Dhruv left, they heard the manager calling out, 'Thank you so much, Sir! Please come again tomorrow! I'm sorry!'

Dhruv was furious about what had just happened. 'How can he throw us out like that?'

'Come on, it's not entirely his fault. You should have at least taken a shower, or changed your T-shirt.'

'But today is a Sunday! And I don't bathe on Sundays, you know that!' Dhruv threw up his hands in exasperation.

It wasn't that Dhruv looked shabby, but Kavya understood the manager's point too. She asked, 'So, what do you want to do now?'

'I don't know.'

Then, with a straight, serious face, he asked, 'Do you just want to go home and have sex?'

Kavya burst out laughing. 'At least don't look this bored when you ask something like this!'

Dhruv smirked. Then feeling disheartened again he asked, 'Then what do you want to do?'

Kavya pondered for a bit before turning to him with an impish smile. 'Do you want to go to a salon with me?'

She knew the answer would be no, but she took her shot anyway.

'What? Why would I want to do that?'

'Because then I can get a hair spa. And then when you play with my hair, it'll be more fun!'

'Yeah, right! When was the last time I did that? Have you seen your hair? If I get my hand anywhere near those wild curls, it'll get lost.'

'But you used to do that, and I miss it!'

Dhruv seemed surprised.

'But then what about my match?'

'Can't you watch it on your mobile phone? Please!'

Seeing Dhruv hesitate, Kavya declared, 'Okay, I've decided. We're going to the salon. You can watch the match on your phone.'

'No, yaar, it's not the same thing! It isn't fun watching it on the mobile phone. See, Kavvu, there are fifty-two Sundays in a year. The chances of Liverpool playing—'

'—I know, I know. The chances of Liverpool playing on a Sunday are a mere 8.8 per cent.'

'Yeah . . .'

'But it's a Sunday and I really want to do something!'

By now, Dhruv wore an expression that Kavya knew very well. It was the face he made when he was almost convinced but was hanging on to the last straw of resistance. With puppy-dog eyes, Kavya squealed, 'Please!'

She knew Dhruv couldn't say no to that. As his shoulders slumped in a gesture of surrender, Kavya smiled triumphantly. She took his hand and they started walking towards the salon.

This girl takes too much advantage of her cuteness, thought Dhruv as he dragged his feet towards the salon.

4

'You have such pretty curls. But why don't you maintain them?' The hairstylist admonished Kavya as he examined her hair.

'Because I don't know how to.'

They were in a plush salon that had smartly dressed hairstylists and jazz music playing softly in the background. Kavya was perched on one of the chairs while Dhruv sat grudgingly on the sofa meant for guests. The match had already started, and he had missed the first few minutes. He clumsily tried to untangle his headphones, but it was difficult to do so while watching the game. He ended up tangling them further, much to his annoyance.

'You should get the keratin treatment and follow it up with a hair spa,' the hairstylist advised. Kavya didn't have a clue about what would be the best thing for her, but she wasn't going to fall for the money-shelling-out trap that was being laid out in the guise of hair care advice. She was only sure that she didn't want both. She turned to Dhruv.

'Listen, Dhruv! Should I get the hair spa done or the keratin treatment?'

Not only did Dhruv have no idea about hair treatment, but he was also bewildered by Kavya seeking his opinion. How was he supposed to know? He was too engrossed in untangling his headphones so he could watch the match in peace.

'If I get the keratin . . .' began Kavya.

'Oh, shit! Almost a goal! It was this close, yaar!' Dhruv held his forefinger and thumb close together to demonstrate the proximity.

Kavya was still staring at him, demanding his attention.

'Get it done,' Dhruv said, too preoccupied.

'Which one should I get done, Dhruv?' Kavya's voice sounded urgent.

'Huh? Get that one—the herbal one.'

'Why not the extra protein one?'

'Get that one, that's the best!'

It was apparent that Dhruv was not paying any attention to what Kavya was saying. He was too absorbed in the match, and rightfully so—it was turning out to be a thrilling contest. Kavya couldn't help feeling irked.

'Fine! You just watch your game!' she snapped, but Dhruv had finally managed to plug in his headphones and couldn't hear her.

'Just do what you think is best,' Kavya told the hairstylist, throwing a miffed look towards Dhruv.

* * *

Barely ten or fifteen minutes after the hairstylist had started working on Kavya's hair Dhruv started shouting and cursing.

'Fuck! Shit!'

So engrossed was he in the game that he seemed to have forgotten where he was.

Kavya was embarrassed. Every person in the salon was looking at Dhruv and then at her. Shocked by the colourful language Dhruv was hurling at his mobile phone, a mother covered her son's ears, condemnation oozing from her body language. The atmosphere at the salon had gone from cheerfully busy to silent and tense in seconds.

'You need to talk to him,' the hairstylist told Kavya, worried that other customers might walk out because of Dhruv. Kavya got up, midway through her spa, half her hair held up with curlers, and walked towards Dhruv.

'Could you please watch your match outside?' Kavya asked Dhruv, her terse manner fully showing the embarrassment she felt.

Dhruv looked up and removed his headphones. He sensed Kavya's discomfort. Then he looked around at the eerily silent salon and the people staring at him, realizing what had happened.

He got up without a word and began to walk out, plugging in his headphones again. But just when he was almost outside, Liverpool missed another chance to score. Frustrated, he cursed loudly again, adding to Kavya's embarrassment.

* * *

'Liverpool will need to pull off something spectacular if they want to stay in the fight for the first three spots in the league . . .'

The commentator was analysing the match as the game entered the final ten minutes. *Why can't Kavya understand that these games are important to me?* Dhruv thought. Things couldn't have got more uncomfortable and irritating for him. Not only was Liverpool down 1-0, he had been forced to watch the game on his mobile phone and been kicked out of the salon as well. To top it all, he was certain that Kavya was pissed off with him.

Dhruv was tired of standing outside on the pavement, and his team's performance only added to his exasperation. *I could've been comfortably sitting at home, having a chilled beer*, he thought. He knew that if the status quo did not change, he would vent his frustration on Kavya and they would end up fighting. He knew he wouldn't be able to help himself.

Hoping against hope, Dhruv crossed his fingers and prayed that Liverpool would at least come up with an equalizer. If not a win, at least a draw. The next five minutes would change the course of the Sunday.

'Goal! Sturridge, you beauty!' Dhruv whooped as Daniel Sturridge scored his second goal in five minutes, giving Liverpool the lead.

Praise the Lord, the impossible had been made possible, Sunday had been saved!

Dhruv put on some victory music and started grooving to it. It was strange how one could go from misery to ecstasy in a matter of minutes. And the reason? Something happening so far, far away. Now in a better mood, Dhruv started thinking more constructively about what had happened in the salon.

Kavya is right. I should be more aware of where I am and what I say. Damn, I must've scarred that kid for life. Dhruv chuckled.

Just then, Kavya walked out of the salon.

'How's it looking?'

Unfortunately for Dhruv, he went with honesty rather than flattery. 'What did you get done? I can't even tell the difference.'

This was enough to annoy Kavya. 'Just like there's no difference in Liverpool's position in the league?'

'Why are you angry?'

'You need to learn how to behave in public, Dhruv.'

'It was an honest mistake, Kavvu. I swear I didn't realize what I was doing.' Dhruv sounded sincere.

'Mistake? Really?' Kavya narrowed her eyes at him. She turned around to walk away, but Dhruv reached out to stop her. However, he ended up stepping on her chappal, almost causing her to fall. She gave him a cold, furious stare.

'Now this was an honest mistake, yaar. Seriously!'

Kavya walked into a store and bought a packet of chips. She munched on them as she walked around inside. Gradually, she calmed down. She realized that she was angry only because she was hungry. Seeing her in a better mood, Dhruv started discussing their dinner plans.

'What do you want to eat? Chinese?'

Kavya scrunched up her face and shook her head in disapproval.

'Mughlai?'

'Too oily!'

'Italian?'

'Too boring!'

'Mexican?'

By now Kavya had finished the packet of chips and realized that she wasn't hungry any more. 'Actually, I'm done.' She looked sheepishly at Dhruv.

'Don't say that, man.'

'Arre, I am full. But I will have a bit with you. Promise.'

Dhruv couldn't hide his disappointment as both of them thought of other places they could go to. Suddenly, Kavya's face lit up.

'Hey, why don't we go to that place you suggested in the morning? The one that serves Kerala food?'

Dhruv perked up instantly, excited about food all over again. 'Good one, Kavvu!' he said, delighted at her suggestion.

How did I forget about that? he wondered as they walked towards the place.

Kavya and Dhruv reached the restaurant only to find a long queue. Dhruv went in and inquired—there was a forty-five-minute wait.

'Are you serious?' It was Kavya's turn to be disappointed.

'You know what? Let's go home and pick up ingredients for some Thai curry on the way. We'll have it with rice. That's the best option!' Dhruv suggested.

'Oh, yeah! And I can make a Snapchat story with instructions on how to make it. Screw you, Megha!'

As they hailed an autorickshaw back to their apartment, Dhruv laughed at how Kavya could be both cute and silly at the same time.

5

Once home, Dhruv and Kavya plonked themselves on the sofa. They were both pretty tired by now. Out of habit, they took out their mobile phones and started looking at their friends' Snapchat stories. Be it Akash's photos of all the fun he was having in Goa or Megha's photos from the splendid Coldplay gig, each passing photo got them a little more agitated. Kavya went to her Snapstory and relived the day. They sat in silence for some time, mentally comparing their Sunday to everyone else's.

That is, until Dhruv reached Kavya's Snapstory. She had put up photos of the brunch, of them watching *Inside Out*, of her at the salon and even photos of them shopping for ingredients for the Thai curry. She had tried very hard to make her day look fun and enjoyable.

It dawned on Dhruv that everyone twisted the truth around, that no one ever had as much fun as they claimed on social media. He turned to Kavya with a smile.

'Kavvu, your day was nothing like what you made it look on your Snapstory.'

'Yeah, so what? I don't want to tell everyone that I had a boring Sunday. Everyone is going places, and look at us. We're just sitting here doing God knows what!'

'Arre, what is this FOMO? I know our day did not go according to plan, but it's not like we had that bad a Sunday. Come on! We had an epic brunch. I got chucked out of a mall and a salon! How often does that happen? We'll be laughing about it for the next two months!' This cheered Kavya up and she broke into a pretty smile.

Dhruv continued. 'Seeing you with those funny red hair clips and watching Sturridge score that goal. Now that made my Sunday perfect. Of course, it could be much cooler and more happening. But isn't that the case with every day? We can't keep comparing our day to others', can we?'

'Hmm . . .' Kavya was lost in thought.

'Besides, we still have that Thai curry to make!' Dhruv desperately tried to help Kavya feel better.

Now that she had come to terms with her Sunday, Kavya realized that she didn't want to go through with the Thai curry plan.

'Listen, Dhruv, can we just order pizza instead? I'm really tired.'

Dhruv heaved a sigh of relief. 'Thank God you said that! Even I am damn tired and was in no mood to slog over the Thai curry.'

Then he remembered. 'Wait, but what about your Snapstory?'

'I don't care.'

'Really? And what will people say?'

'Other people can go to hell! It might sound lame, but you know what I really want to do? I want to have some pizza with a glass of red wine, finish watching *Inside Out* and then just go to sleep.'

They gave each other a knowing smile.

'That sounds perfect,' Dhruv replied.

'It sounds like our kind of Sunday,' added Kavya.

'Exactly.'

So Dhruv and Kavya ordered in pizza, had some wine and finished watching *Inside Out*. Some would call this the perfect end to a week and the best start to a new one. Kavya even managed to take a lot of photos for Snapchat during dinner and the movie and showed all her friends that you didn't have to play large to have fun.

As she snuggled in with Dhruv later, she took the final snap for the day: '100 per cent Dhruv and Kavya'.

It was in Dhruv's arms that she found happiness and felt secure. With him, everything seemed just right.

HAVE A NICE DAY!

1

It was a typical Monday morning. Dhruv opened all the windows and pulled back the curtains. A gentle breeze blew into the house. The chirping of birds floated into the room.

Dhruv felt a sense of calm as he made coffee for both Kavya and himself, then read the newspaper and watered the plants. He even messaged his mother a cheery 'Good morning, Ma!'

At the other end of the spectrum was Kavya. While Dhruv moved about outside and finished his chores, she lay in bed, drooling from the side of her mouth, blissfully unaware of the fact that she was running really late. She was definitely not a morning person. But as they say, opposites attract. It was probably the reason why Dhruv and she functioned so well as a team. Dhruv's coffee was yet to have an effect on Kavya, so he decided to start getting dressed. As he entered the room to get his things, he saw Kavya sleepily move towards the bathroom.

'Hello! No, no, no, no . . .' Dhruv grabbed her just as she was about to enter the bathroom.

Kavya struggled with him, begged and made a puppy-dog face and then begged some more. 'Please, please, just let me go first.'

'How is this fair? I got up first, switched on the geyser and made coffee. I even woke you up! You remember? You remember that, don't you?'

Seeing that her puppy-dog expression wasn't working, Kavya appealed more desperately. 'I know, I know! But I have my weekly meeting at 9 a.m. and Manoj Sir will kill me if I am late again. And you can go to work even at 1 p.m., *na*?'

Dhruv was a student of mathematics, a subject most people dread. But he was good at it and was seeking a university grant that would help him complete his research paper and get his degree. He did go to an office, but he was his own boss, which is why his hours were flexible.

It was discipline and a strict schedule that had enabled him to come so far.

'Hey, no! I also have to leave on time, right? What is this? You need to be more disciplined, Kavya.'

'Okay, Daddy, next time!'

'I really wish I was. If you were my daughter . . .'

'If I was your daughter? Really? Isn't it weird for you to say that considering the things we were doing at 3 a.m. because of which I woke up late?' The grumpiness on Kavya's face was now replaced by a naughty smile.

'Yeah, okay, okay . . . fine,' said Dhruv, trying to banish the image from his mind. Now that he thought about it, it sounded disgusting.

'It sounded fine in my head. But when I said it, I too . . .'

He shook his head and realized that they were only wasting time and getting delayed further.

'Wait! Why am I explaining myself? I am getting late!' he said, shoving Kavya away from the bathroom door.

As Kavya stood there stubbornly, Dhruv decided to trick her. 'Fun fact, fun fact, fun fact!'

Kavya looked at him, wondering what he had to say.

'Do you know, "Daddy" is the most searched keyword on Pornhub? You know what it is in India? Tell me quick!'

'I don't know!'

'Guess, guess . . .'

'Boob, maybe?'

As she thought about it, Kavya didn't realize that she had let Dhruv enter the bathroom and close the door. The moment she registered this, she banged on the door angrily.

'Dhruv!'

'*Bhabhi*!' he shouted back.

'What?'

'Bhabhi, sister-in-law, is the most searched-for keyword . . .'

'Yeah, okay. Thanks for telling me that. Now come out fast, I need to go!'

Just then her stomach rumbled. She decided to prepare some breakfast while Dhruv bathed. She knocked on the door. 'Would you like scrambled eggs?'

'Can you make French toast, please?' he called out over the sound of the shower.

'No, it takes a lot of time and I need to iron my clothes as well.'

'I'll iron your clothes. Please make French toast! It'll only take two more minutes. It's Monday and I need an extra boost, Kavya Kulkarni!'

'Yeah, fine, glutton!' she gave in. *Why had she even bothered to ask?*

'*Tamma, tamma loge . . .*' Dhruv sang happily inside the bathroom. He had been singing that song all through the previous day and it was really getting on Kavya's nerves. Annoyed, she shouted.

'Stop singing that song!'

Dhruv started laughing at how much it bugged her.

'It's stuck in my head too! I need to get it out.'

* * *

Later, as Kavya applied lipstick in front of the mirror, one thing was certain—she was furious. She put on the earrings that Dhruv had given her for her birthday, the ones she loved. But right now her mind was only focused on the rage boiling within her.

Dhruv came in, still humming the song, completely unaware of the trouble he was in.

'These are really nice, Kavvu,' he said, taking a huge bite of a French toast.

Kavya whirled around and held up the clothes Dhruv had ironed for her.

'What is this, Dhruv?'

'What happened?'

'This, can't you see this?'

Kavya pointed to a large burn mark on the sleeve of the shirt he had ironed. 'Are you blind?'

'How did that happen?'

'You should have checked the iron before using it! Now I have to wear this crumpled shirt and go!'

That's when she saw Dhruv's dirty clothes and wet towel tossed carelessly across the chair. 'How many times have I asked you not to leave dirty clothes here?'

Dhruv tried to defuse the situation. 'Wear something else, Kavya.'

'I don't have anything else to wear. Nothing else is ironed. And I'm super late anyway.' She threw the wet towel at him and stormed out of the room.

'So selfish, Dhruv! Just finish your stupid toast. Have a nice day!' With this, she slammed the door and left.

Dhruv turned around and noticed something that made him feel even worse. In her hurry to reach work on time, Kavya had forgotten to eat the breakfast she had made for herself!

2

Kavya got off the autorickshaw and ran across the road towards her office.

'Oh, Madam!' someone yelled behind her. Kavya turned to see her autorickshaw driver glaring at her.

'Oh, shit!' She'd forgotten to pay him in her hurry. She ran back, apologized and paid the man.

Then she made a dash for it again. A car brushed past her just as she reached the other end. Kavya thanked her lucky stars at being able to get away with the reckless rushing.

Never again will I be late, she promised herself—just as she had done hundreds of times before.

She rushed into the lift of the glass-paned building that was her office. The lift doors had just closed when she pressed the button. They opened again. The people inside stared at her impatiently. Everyone was in a hurry.

'Seventh floor, please,' she said, feeling conscious about the fact that her shirt wasn't ironed.

Minutes later, Kavya knocked on the door of the conference room and entered, her eyes fixed on the floor. For the second time in ten minutes, she felt people's eyes on her, staring and judging. She adjusted her shirt nervously.

'Kavya, you're late again?' Her boss sounded exasperated. It seemed to be more of a statement than a question. His face reflected a mix of disappointment and anger.

'Have a seat,' he said, shaking his head in disapproval as the meeting resumed.

But there was no chair for Kavya and she had to keep standing—like a child sent to a corner to be punished. She felt humiliated as her boss spoke to the rest of the team and she wasn't included in the discussion. She grew angrier and angrier at Dhruv as she blamed his demand for French toast for her day spiralling into a haphazard mess.

* * *

Meanwhile, Dhruv too was not having the best of days. He needed to get his passport renewed to travel outside the country and complete his research. But bureaucratic red tape and inefficient government officials made this task way more complicated than it should have been. He was still shouting at someone on the phone when he stepped into his office.

'How many times should I send you the identification documents? I've sent them thrice already!'

Akash, Dhruv's friend and batchmate, was trying to fix his computer and had his head almost inside it. He jumped, hit his head on the computer, and looked up, annoyed.

'The permanent address is in Delhi. I have already told you this. Please sort it out quickly. Passport renewal should not take so much time. All right, thank you.'

Akash could make out that Dhruv was really upset.

'What's up? What's wrong? Is Uber on surge pricing again?'

'Don't start with me, man . . .'

'Fine!' Akash said, dropping the topic. 'FYI, my RAM isn't working, so I'm busy anyway. Okay?'

'It's just been a shitty morning, yaar. First I had a fight with Kavya over a stupid thing. And now this whole passport renewal mess . . .'

Akash dropped all his work and turned towards him.

'There's something about girls, no? Saloni is also very weird in the morning . . .'

'Dude! When will you stop comparing your one-night stands with my two-year-old relationship?'

Annoyed, Akash got up and pretended to look for something.

'You know what? I have something for you. Where is it? Where is it?'

He put his hand inside the shell of the computer and pulled it out—his middle finger raised.

'Here it is! Isn't it yours?'

'Funny, dude. Very mature,' Dhruv replied sarcastically, equally mad at his friend.

Akash turned back to his work.

'Listen, Akash . . .' Dhruv said. Akash ignored him.

'Arre, Akash, just listen.'

Akash finally turned around.

'What is it?'

'Did you get an email from Stockholm?'

Both of them had applied for a grant there and were awaiting a response.

'Not yet. You?'

'Nope.'

Dhruv sighed and got down to work.

* * *

In another part of the city, Kavya was battling her own set of issues. Her boss was screaming at her from inside his cabin.

'Kavya, did you find out why the Eternity Mall guys haven't replied about the pricing?'

Everyone on the floor could hear him.

'I'm just following up on that, Sir!'

Kavya frantically combed through her emails but couldn't find the one she really needed to.

Why can't I find that stupid email? I swear I sent it!

Kirtana, her colleague and friend who sat next to her, was listening.

'When did you send it?'

'Sometime last week. I marked you on the email, didn't I?'

Kavya looked up to find Kirtana staring at her with a puzzled expression.

'Kavya, why are you wearing one earring?'

Kavya felt her ears and panicked.

'Did you drop the other one somewhere?'

Kavya abandoned her search for the missing email and started looking for the earring. She dropped to her knees to look under her desk and on the floor.

'Shit, shit, shit! I can't lose these! These are the earrings Dhruv gave me on my birthday!'

Kirtana joined her in the search, but to no avail. Dejected, Kavya started to get up and hit her head against the table. She fell back to the floor, close to bursting into tears. She wondered if this day could get any worse.

The day did get worse for Dhruv . . .

'The mail from Stockholm is here!' Akash shouted in excitement. Dhruv reached for his mobile phone and began to scan his inbox.

'Yes! White chicks, white chicks, whatcha gonna do, whatcha gonna do, when I come for you?' Akash parodied the *Bad Boys* theme song while doing a crazy jig. He turned towards Dhruv and stopped abruptly. His eyes on his mobile phone, Dhruv looked pale.

'What's up, man?'

'I didn't get through.'

Akash had known Dhruv for years. He was easily one of the smartest and most hard-working people he knew—not only in his batch, but in the whole college. It was shocking to think that Akash had got through and Dhruv hadn't.

'Yeah, right, don't bullshit me,' Akash said in disbelief, grabbing Dhruv's mobile phone to read the email.

'I regret to inform you that your paper, 'The Injectivity of Isometric Numbers', has not been accepted for presentation at the 27th Nordic Congress . . .'

'Enough! Stop reading!'

Akash looked sadly at Dhruv's distraught face.

'My paper is not getting accepted,' Dhruv said softly.

Akash wanted to comfort him in some way, but he didn't know how to.

'It's okay, Dhruv, I'm sure we'll figure something out.'

'If my paper is not getting cleared, how the hell will I get my degree?' Dhruv held his head in his hands. Today was just not his day. Just not his day . . .

But it wasn't Kavya's either.

'That does not matter!' Kavya's boss shouted at her—for the third time that day, his mood at its worst. And it wasn't even lunchtime yet.

'How could you send the client our internal costing?' Her boss was shocked at Kavya's blunder.

'You were supposed to send them the quotes. No wonder they've not replied! They'll come back with some shitty pricing now that they know our costs!'

'I know, Sir. I must've forwarded the wrong attachment.' Kavya rucfully bit her tongue even as no words escaped her mouth. She felt horrible.

'This is such a huge order for the company, Kavya. Why couldn't you have been more careful? What's happened to you? This is the second time in this month that such a thing has happened. This is some seriously shoddy work, Kavya. Really shoddy!'

'I'm sorry, Sir. I'm really very sorry . . .'

As they say, when it rains it pours.

Dhruv had been brooding for nearly half an hour when Akash decided to take things into his own hands. He couldn't bear to see Dhruv so dejected.

'Dhruv, cheer up, man! It's no big deal if you didn't get through. There are so many options out there. There's Illinois, Ohio, Toronto and so many others!'

'But those are all the tough options, and you know that. This was the easy backup and even that didn't work out.'

Akash knew that Dhruv was right. There was no rationale or logic he could use to refute that. So he turned to the easiest and most sure-shot method he knew to cheer a guy up. He went to his cupboard.

'Let me get you something.'

Dhruv had no patience for whatever Akash was up to. There was tremendous pressure on him and he had to figure out what to do.

'No, Akash, don't joke now. I'm not in the mood, seriously.'

'Wait, wait, wait!' Akash opened the cupboard. 'Ta-da!'

In his hand was a half-full bottle of the finest Scotch whisky Chivas Regal had to offer. Dhruv was aghast. Not only was it a very expensive bottle of liquor, but he also wondered how the hell was it in the office.

'What the—!'

Akash beamed with pride as though he had distilled and brewed the Scotch himself. 'Look at this beauty! Tantalizing, alluring and tempting golden juice, waiting to trickle down your throat, spreading warmth—the kind that radiates from your stomach and releases all tension and kills all grief!'

Dhruv grinned. It was incredible what a good friend can and will do for you.

'Only if you were this romantic when it came to a girl, you would've found someone who could bear the thought of being with you!'

The tension evaporated and both of them burst out laughing.

'You're too much of a miser to buy this bottle, I know that for sure. Where on earth did you steal it from?' Dhruv asked his friend.

'I am not a miser, I'm just underpaid. Don't tell anyone. This is Rao Sir's special stash that he thinks he's hidden very well. Whenever I feel low or when things aren't working out, I sneak this bottle out, pour a bit of it into my coffee mug, mix it with Coke and pretend it's black coffee—one of life's easiest hacks!'

Dhruv felt amused. 'But doesn't he find out that someone has been drinking from this bottle?'

'Dude, don't underestimate how cunning I am, please! I keep refilling it with Coke and water from time to time. This way, not only do I maintain the volume of whisky but also its colour and consistency. Ingenious!'

Akash looked at Dhruv. 'Come! Let's have a couple of drinks. We'll fix your mood.'

Dhruv smiled.

'You know what? Let's have biryani! Let me order some,' Akash added.

'Yeah,' said Dhruv, pleased at the thought of food. Life wasn't going his way anyway.

'Keema or Afghani?'

'Any, you're paying anyway.'

'Yeah, my treat.'

As much as Dhruv was smiling and playing along with Akash's attempts at cheering him up, not getting through Stockholm was still gnawing away at his happiness. He was sitting there, still brooding, when his gaze fell on a photo of Kavya on his desk. She was sticking her tongue out and holding up a plate of freshly cut mangoes. Dhruv couldn't help but smile. Kavya radiated warmth and comfort. As long as she was with him, he felt strong enough to take on any challenge life might throw at him.

And as suddenly as it had come, the heaviness in his heart lifted and the haze in his mind cleared.

'Listen, Akash, can you please make that three biryanis?'

'Are you sure?'

'Yes.'

'Okay, I'm ordering the kebabs as well.'

Dhruv's heart was filled with gratitude. There were still a lot of things worth smiling about . . .

* * *

Kavya was sitting at her desk and wallowing in sorrow and self-pity. There seemed to be nothing that could pull her out of the slump. Everything seemed to be in vain.

'Madam, there's a parcel from Dhruv Sir for you.' The office boy's voice jolted Kavya out of her thoughts. She stared at him, still in a daze, then rose and walked slowly to the reception.

The receptionist seemed to have gone for lunch, but a white plastic bag sat on the desk with her name scribbled on it. She opened it to find a plastic box with a note stuck to it:

I know I don't deserve a gold medal in ironing clothes. But I have a decent track record in gluttony. Sending you some of me, packed in a box. =) Dhruv

Kavya opened the box and was delighted at the sight and fragrance of the keema biryani. Her stomach growled, begging for food. She realized how hungry she was and headed to her desk with the packet.

Halfway, Kavya turned around. If she took the biryani to her desk, she would have to offer it to everyone, and she was in no mood to share Dhruv's love. Instead, she stepped out to the exit staircase—no one would bother her there.

Kavya couldn't wait. She was famished. She wolfed down the biryani, her mind focused only on satisfying her hunger. Once her stomach started feeling full, she remembered that she should at least thank Dhruv. She took out her mobile phone and took a selfie, making a face while eating the biryani. She sent him the picture.

Thank you. I really needed this right now. And sorry about the morning. I was rude. Love you! ☺ *<3*

A few seconds later, she received a reply.

It's all right. You were stressed out. And why aren't you eating at your table? Don't want to share your food? :P
Also, Biryani Monster is looking really cute.

Then another message:

And by the way, I did not get through to the Stockholm Conference. Bad day :(

Kavya felt guilty. She had been rude, even yelled at Dhruv for a small mistake and then called him selfish before slamming the door on his face. Yet, he was doing things to make her feel better and special. If anything, he was the exact opposite of selfish. She had to make up for the morning, and fast. Finishing her biryani, Kavya fished out her drawing book and got down to work.

3

Dhruv and Akash lounged in their chairs, leaning back and gazing at the ceiling with their legs propped up on the desk. It had been a splendid afternoon. They had stuffed themselves with biryani and had more whisky than they should have, while gossiping and talking about the good old days, girls, movies and much more.

The lethargy was intense. Dhruv had been trying to convince himself to get up and work but had not moved an inch. He needed to get some work done or he would feel bad later and not be able to sleep. Finally, after what seemed like ages, he mustered all his willpower and managed to get up. Half the battle won, Dhruv stood staring at the formulae scribbled on the whiteboard above his desk.

Hearing Dhruv get up, Akash too woke up from his slumber.

'We ate too much for our own good, didn't we?' he mumbled, his lips barely moving, his eyes droopy.

'Yeah, and drank a lot too.'

'Whisky, biryani and kebabs. Such a perfect afternoon!' Akash smiled contentedly.

Dhruv smiled back. He felt much better, all thanks to Akash. He had surrounded himself with great people and was feeling really thankful for them.

'I know. We just needed some sad ghazals by Jagjit Singh and we would have a *mehfil* in the office!'

'And babes, Dhruv. Don't forget the babes.' Dhruv was about to give him a cold look of disapproval when he remembered all that Akash had done for him that day. A smile broke across his face. *Just Akash being Akash*, he thought. He wouldn't change him for the world.

Dhruv took out his mobile phone from his pocket to check for messages from Kavya. There were none. This was very unlike her— usually she would have immediately called and comforted him.

He was banking on her to take away all the despair inside him. *She must be caught up with something. I'm sure her ass of a boss is giving her a tough time and keeping her away from her mobile phone.*

Just as he was about to put his mobile phone back into his pocket, it beeped. It was a message from Kavya. Dhruv was already smiling. Just a small reminder of her presence was enough to make him feel happy and warm.

But before he could read the message, his phone beeped again—and again and again—almost twenty times.

'What the hell!' exclaimed Dhruv. He opened the chat to see that Kavya had sent him multiple photos. He was amazed at what he saw. She had drawn a photo story for him!

Once upon a time, there was a boy called Dhruv who was very nervous because he was racing the fastest boy in town.

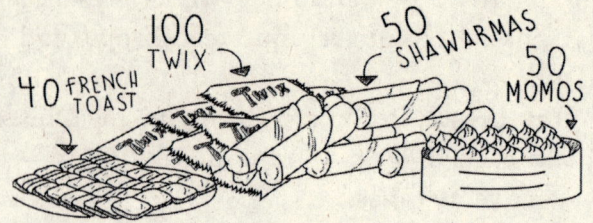

The winner would get 100 Twix bars, fifty shawarma rolls, fifty momos and forty French toasts.

Given that all of these were among his favourite things, Dhruv was in no mood to lose.

But how do you defeat the fastest boy in town?

The race started, and at the halfway mark Dhruv started to feel very tired. He couldn't run any more.

Just then, Dhruv heard somebody cheering him on from the sidelines.

Amidst the crowd, his eyes locked in on his best friend, the Biryani Monster, who was cheering for him with all his might.

That encouraged Dhruv and he started to believe in himself. He ran and ran like he had never run before.

Before he knew it, he had defeated the fastest boy in town and was celebrating his victory with his best friend.

As the two of them hugged, his best friend whispered something into his ear that he would never forget: *You will never walk alone.*

The last image tugged at Dhruv's heart. He was overwhelmed and smiled brightly.

He wished he could pull Kavya close and squeeze her into a bear hug that very instant. He wanted to tell her how much he loved her, write odes to her, serenade her and build monuments as a testament to his love for her.

But for now, a simple gesture would do. And he had just the thing in mind.

4

After a taxing day at work, Kavya took a cab back home. She wondered if Dhruv would be home. As she reached their apartment, she noticed that the door was slightly ajar and there was loud music playing inside. Puzzled, she stepped into the living room.

Her eyes widened with surprise and joy on seeing Dhruv dancing away merrily, holding the portable speaker in his hand. He had his sunglasses on; there were two or three long gold chains around his neck and one earring stuck to his ear in complete hip-hop style. Kavya brought her hand up to her mouth to stifle her laughter.

'What the hell are you doing, Dhruv?'

Dhruv jumped.

'What the fuck! You scared me, Kavya!' He grinned and turned up the volume.

'Bloody Biryani Monster, come here!' He laughed and pulled her close.

Such a crazy, cute boy! Kavya thought. She watched him dance, noticing his movements, his clothes, his accessories . . .

'Are you wearing my jewellery, Dhruv?'

'I'm Bappi Da, bro!' Dhruv shouted over the music.

Kavya's gaze fell on the single earring Dhruv was wearing.

'Is that my earring?' she exclaimed, relief flooding her body.

'I was so scared that I'd lost it. I spent hours looking for it at work!'

'Yeah, you forgot it here in the morning. Why are you talking so much? Dance with me!'

'Tamma tamma loge' was playing on loop. The song bugged the hell out of Kavya, but not right now—she was too busy doting over Dhruv at the moment.

'This is how you get a song out of your head!' Dhruv yelled, grinning.

'Thank God! I was feeling so bad . . .'

'Now stop talking so much and please just start dancing, Kavya!'

Kavya smiled, kicked off her shoes and joined in, forgetting everything as they swayed to the music.

After fifteen minutes of dancing with reckless abandon, Dhruv knew the coast was clear and it wasn't 'too soon' any more. 'Your shirt is looking really nice,' he said impishly, poking Kavya for a reaction, knowing he would get away with it.

Kavya pretended to slap him really hard and he turned a full 360 degrees, pretending to fall down because of the impact. He got up, reduced the volume and then stopped and stared at Kavya with a knowing and grateful smile. Kavya, too, stopped dancing, looked into his eyes and smiled. It was the perfect moment.

'I'm sorry, Kavya.'

She let out a laugh and jumped towards him with her arms wide open. Dhruv picked her up and embraced her, wrapping her tightly in his arms and swinging her around. It had been a long, hard day for both of them, but now everything was good, all was well.

5

They were lying in bed, doing their usual chit-chat. Kavya was telling Dhruv about her blunder at work. Dhruv listened, playing with her hair.

'But how did this happen?' Dhruv was astonished and burst out laughing.

'Don't laugh, Momo! You know I didn't . . .'

'How can I help it? It's too damn funny, Kavvu!'

'You have no idea how boring it gets at work. And I was distracted anyway. I had told myself that I would not stay on Facebook for more than fifteen minutes. But then I saw this really cool article that talked about ten places to visit in under five thousand bucks.'

'What? That's it?'

'Yes, just five thousand bucks, Dhruv! We could do one every month! So I started reading the article. And then I started planning holidays with you to those places. My concentration said, "Bye-bye, Kavya! See you later!"'

Dhruv sympathized but also wanted to give her practical advice like he felt he should.

'But you can't be on Facebook when you are working, Kavvu. It's as simple as that! But, wait, who am I to give you any advice? I'm also on Facebook the whole day . . .'

And then he remembered.

'Hey, you know what? Download this app called Self Control. Akash uses it all the time. You feed in your work hours and it blocks Facebook during that period. That way you can't access Facebook in those hours even if you don't delete Facebook or the Self Control app.'

To Kavya this seemed like a drastic measure. 'That will make my day a million times more boring, Dhruv!'

'But you will also not make mistakes like these then.'

'Hmm . . . that's true,' Kavya agreed half-heartedly, twirling a curl around her finger. It seemed too much to ask.

'Thanks . . . Daddy!' she said, trying to make Dhruv uncomfortable.

But Dhruv was not somebody to be embarrassed so easily. He took advantage of the situation and turned towards Kavya with a creepy smile. 'You know, that word really turns me on. It really, really does . . .'

'Shut up, Dhruv!' Kavya laughed, pushing him away.

'You know what I did after lunch today?' she said, changing the topic.

'What?'

'I ordered *Fifty Shades of Grey* as a gift for my boss—anonymously!'

Dhruv's eyes widened.

'What! Are you mad or what, Kavya? Like seriously?'

'Madness, as you know, is like gravity. All you need is a little push!'

'Batman!' Dhruv laughed, recognizing the quote immediately.

'What's Batman, Dhruv? Say *The Dark Knight*.'

'By the way, your boss can figure out who it's from. All he has to do is register one complaint. You're so screwed, Kavya Kulkarni!'

'Are you serious? Oh, no!' She couldn't really afford to mess things up with her boss any more.

'Do something about it! What's the point of your PhD? Put it to good use and think of a solution!

'Just cancel the order, you idiot!' Dhruv said lightly.

Kavya couldn't believe the solution could be that simple.

'Oh, yeah! That was so easy! Why did I not think of it?' she said, laughing with relief.

'So, what's for dinner?'

'I'm not that hungry.'

'No, don't say that!'

This couldn't happen. Dhruv was always hungry. How could Kavya not be too?

'I'll just reheat the French toast from the morning and eat them,' Kavya said.

'That's all gone,' Dhruv pointed to his belly.

'Dhruv!'

'What could I do? It was so tasty, and I was really hungry. So I ate it,' he said in a very matter-of-fact way.

'What do we eat now?' Kavya started pouting again.

'I have an idea! Do you want to eat some pasta?'

'Are you making it?' Kavya was in no mood to cook.

'Yes, I'll make it, you sloth bear.'

'Okay, cool, then I'll have some!'

Then, feeling sorry for Dhruv having to do everything, she added, 'I'll come and help you chop the vegetables.'

No sooner had she said that than Kavya changed her mind.

'Actually, no. I'm not going to do that. You do all the work, and I'll just talk to you and distract you.'

'Thought so!' Dhruv smirked. 'I was wondering how my sloth bear had offered to work?'

And then they cooked, talked about their day, and planned to go for all those under-five thousand-rupee vacations.

Just before sleeping, Dhruv asked Kavya for her sketchbook and carefully tore out the last page of the photo story she'd made for him.

He got up and stuck it on the section of the wall dedicated to Kavya's sketches, drawings and doodles. For him, it was her most precious work yet. It wasn't just the nicest and most beautiful gift she had given him—it was the best thing anyone had ever done for him. He

felt very special. A sign above the pictures said
'Not for Sale'. Yes, none of this was for sale. He
was glad that there were some things money
couldn't buy.

Dhruv returned to bed, kissed Kavya good
night and cuddled her. He fell asleep looking at
the picture on the wall.

GOOD NIGHT

1

Kavya and Dhruv lay in bed, with Dhruv listening closely as she read aloud from Roald Dahl's *The Wish*.

' . . . and the next thing he saw was this bare hand of his going right into the middle of a great glistening mass of black, and he gave one piercing cry as it touched. Outside in the sunshine, far away behind the house, the mother was looking for her son.'

'Wasn't it nice?' she asked him as she closed the book.

'I didn't really get the end,' Dhruv said, snuggling up to her.

Dhruv had almost fallen asleep when he noticed that Kavya was reading Roald Dahl, one of his favourite authors. He had asked her to read out loud to him, as he often did. She had obliged, as she always did. Kavya loved reading to Dhruv, especially because it would make him wrap his arms around her and give her his undivided attention. A discussion involving their interpretations and perspectives of the book usually followed.

'I think it is about how children are busy with their own adventures, and how we grow up but our parents keep looking for that little child, or something like that . . .' Kavya mused.

There was a long pause. Dhruv's face was scrunched up in thought as he pondered over what Kavya had just said. Kavya, meanwhile, was getting ready to sleep. She took off her bracelet and kept the book on the bedside table.

'That does sound nice, doesn't it?' said Dhruv. 'Thank you, Kavvu. No one could have said it better.' He kissed her tenderly. 'Uff! Now I feel like calling my mom!' he moaned.

'I know, right?' Even Kavya was missing her mother.

'All right, I'm going to sleep now.'

'Me too,' Kavya said, picking up her phone. 'I'm going to set an alarm for tomorrow. I have a long day.'

'Set it for when you have to wake up, and not an hour before that.'

Kavya was a snoozer. She had a habit of hitting the snooze button at least four or five times before finally waking up. This meant that her process of waking up started more than an hour before she actually got out of bed.

'But you know that I need an hour to wake up!'

'But it disturbs my sleep. You keep hitting the snooze button every fifteen minutes. Thirty seconds after you hit snooze, you're sleeping like a log. But I don't work like that. From the first time the alarm rings, I'm up. And every time it rings, I get more and more annoyed. Then I feel sleepy the whole day. Please, Kavya!'

Dhruv had tried his best not to let his annoyance show. She realized it would be difficult for a light sleeper like Dhruv to adjust to this.

'Okay, okay. Sorry, Momo. I'll set an alarm for thirty minutes before I need to wake up. Okay?'

But thoughts of her boss shouting at her made her panic.

'Sorry, sorry. I'll set it for forty minutes before I have to wake up.' She reconsidered. 'No! Forty-five minutes. Please!'

Dhruv could not stay mad when Kavya was being so cute. In an instant, all his irritation vanished and he started laughing. He couldn't help it. Kavya was so animated when she was upset or worried.

'Okay, Baba. Set it for whenever you want!' he said affectionately and pulled her into a tighter embrace, kissing her cheeks.

'Good night. I love you!'

Kavya smiled. 'Good night! I love you too,' she said.

The world felt warm and safe in Dhruv's embrace.

Dhruv moved ever so slightly, and there it was—the perfect position to curl up and sleep. Kavya had already fallen asleep with the sheet pulled over her head.

* * *

Slap! Smack! Whack!

Kavya was jolted out of her sleep.

'No! No! No!' Dhruv shouted angrily.

'Oh, no! Don't tell me this is happening again!' Kavya wailed.

They had forgotten to check whether all the windows were shut. One had somehow remained open and numerous mosquitoes had made their way in.

Kavya switched on the light by her bedside. Dhruv was lashing out at the mosquitoes like a madman.

'What breed of mosquito is this? Immune to everything! I've tried mosquito coils, mosquito repellent creams, everything! Nothing works!' Dhruv was sleepy and frustrated.

Smack! Kavya randomly slapped her hands together and two mosquitoes lay splattered on her palms.

'Yay! I killed two!' She flicked the dead insects off her hands and sneakily wiped the blood on Dhruv's T-shirt.

'Amazing! Congratulations, Kavya. Two down, 200 to go!'

'Momo, please let's just cover our heads and go to sleep. I have work tomorrow. And you know I have to get up extra early.'

'All right, I'll try.' Dhruv sighed and killed another two or three mosquitoes.

Kavya switched off the lights and they covered themselves with the sheet. But two or three minutes later, the mosquitoes had found their way inside the sheet too. Dhruv threw it off and switched on the lights.

'Kavvu! Kavya! Please get up. Please do something. Get up!' Dhruv almost lifted her out of the bed.

'Ughhhhhh! You're not going to let me sleep either!'

Kavya knew that this tantrum was not going to end unless she found a fix for the problem.

'I am going to find a solution to this once and for all,' she declared and grabbed her mobile phone from the bedside table for some quick Internet research.

Smack!

'Ouch!' Kavya yelled in pain and stared at Dhruv. He was so hell-bent on killing the mosquitoes that he hadn't realized he had actually hit Kavya on the arm.

Something had to be done.

2

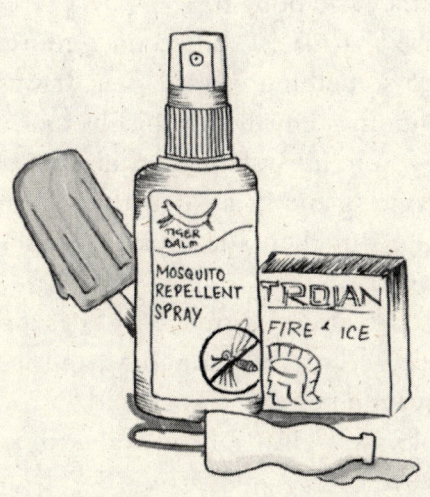

'That will be Rs 380, Ma'am,' a tired pharmacist told Kavya. After trying every home remedy that the Internet had suggested, and failing miserably, Kavya and Dhruv had decided to walk to the nearest pharmacy and buy the best mosquito cream they could get their hands on.

'What? How can it be Rs 380? All we bought was mosquito cream and two ice creams!'

Kavya started checking the prices of the items they had bought.

The pharmacist shifted uncomfortably and pushed something towards her. It was a pack of condoms. Dhruv sheepishly took out the money from his wallet and paid the man.

Kavya glanced at it and couldn't help smiling. But then she took a second look at the cover.

'What is this, Dhruv? Why does it say "Fire and Ice"?' Kavya was laughing and looking at Dhruv with her eyebrows raised.

'I know, right?' Dhruv said with a twinkle in his eyes.

'Why would anyone want to use this? Especially in Mumbai where it is already so hot and humid?'

'We'll find out!'

'We,' Kavya clarified, 'are not using this.'

'Why not?'

'Because why would I want to feel hot or cold down there?'

'Let's try at least,' Dhruv said, but Kavya was still shaking her head.

Meanwhile, the pharmacist had been looking from Dhruv to Kavya and back throughout the exchange, part embarrassed and part shocked by the frank exchange.

Dhruv put his arm around Kavya. 'What's the worst thing that could happen? I'll go to the doctor . . .'

'Okay,' Kavya said picking up all the packets from the counter. Dhruv was still talking.

'. . . and say that I was having sex wearing a "Fire and Ice" condom. And it burnt all my pubic hair!'

Kavya walked out. She had been embarrassed enough and the pharmacist was giving them a creepy smile.

'Good night, Sir!' he called out after them.

'Hey, stop walking so fast!' Kavya told Dhruv after a few minutes.

'I'm not walking fast, you are walking slowly.' Dhruv was enjoying his orange ice cream.

Kavya caught up with him and offered him her chocolate ice cream, which he took.

'Mine is better,' he said.

'Can I try it?'

Dhruv hated sharing food. 'Sure, do you want anything else? A back massage or . . .' he teased Kavya.

Just then, someone in a passing autorickshaw hit Dhruv on the head. Both the ice creams fell from his hands.

Dhruv was stunned. 'What the hell was that?'

'What the hell was that!' shrieked Kavya.

'Some idiot just smacked me on the head!' said Dhruv in disbelief as he touched his head gingerly. He shouted at the autorickshaw. 'I will screw your happiness, you piece of shit!'

This was followed by more profanities in Hindi. Kavya started laughing. Rarely did the stereotypical Delhi boy in Dhruv rear his head.

But when he was angry and swearing, the Delhi effect showed clearly.

'Oye, Mr Delhi 2016, relax!'

'What, yaar! Who was that?'

Just then, the autorickshaw turned around and headed back towards them. Dhruv panicked. Kavya was with him and that was a vulnerability. He grabbed her hand and started running in the opposite direction.

'Shit! He's taking a U-turn! Run, Kavya, run!'

Kavya jogged with him. But she didn't feel threatened at all. In fact, she was laughing at how scared Dhruv was.

'Shitface! Where are you running off to?' someone shouted from the autorickshaw. The voice was strangely familiar. Dhruv turned and saw a face peeking out. The autorickshaw stopped a little ahead of them and a guy stepped out.

'Karan! What on earth are you doing here, man?' Dhruv exclaimed with joy. 'How are you?'

'How are you doing?' Karan grinned. The two hugged and slapped each other's backs while Kavya watched with a smile.

'How are you, man?' asked Karan again.

'All good, dude! You tell me . . .' Dhruv was pleasantly surprised to see his childhood friend.

'Nothing, man. Just here in the city for a few more hours—like four more hours. Came in just for a day for some work. Will head back tomorrow morning,' Karan explained. 'You tell me, how are you? Offering private tuitions like Mishra?'

'I'm seriously thinking of doing that,' Dhruv laughed. As mathematics students, a lot of their batchmates provided private tuitions to earn some extra money. One of their friends, Amol Mishra, had got so frustrated with exams and writing papers and theses that he took up tuitions as a full-time profession.

'By the way, this is my girlfriend, Kavya.' Dhruv gestured towards Kavya.

'And Kavya, this is Karan, my childhood friend from Delhi. He shat in his shorts in the second grade!'

'Good to know.' Kavya laughed awkwardly.

Dhruv loved embarrassing people. In fact, one could say that making people feel awkward was one of his hobbies. But Karan wasn't one to hold back. After all, he was one of Dhruv's oldest friends and knew a lot of stories about him too.

'Thanks, man. That is the best introduction I've ever got! And as long as we're at it, hi, Kavya! This is my moronic friend, Dhruv, who got caught by a teacher in the fifth grade for stealing a second grader's lunch. When the teacher was scolding him, he couldn't say anything in his defence because he had stuffed so much food into his mouth that neither was he able to talk nor was he able to chew.'

All of them broke into laughter.

'That's horrible, Dhruv!' Kavya admonished him playfully. 'So you've been stealing food since you were a kid!'

'See, I was always this cute!' Dhruv winked at Kavya.

'No, you were always so fat,' Karan interrupted, 'that you needed so much food to stuff your face—'

'Come on, Karan, that boy's mother made the best food. Tell her, dude! Even you know that, so it was justified. Kavya, you would have done the same thing!' Dhruv explained earnestly, a smile still lingering in his eyes.

'No, I wouldn't have,' Kavya argued.

'You look even better in real life than in pictures, Kavya,' said Karan, turning his attention towards her.

Kavya blushed. 'Thanks!'

'But if you don't mind me asking,' Karan continued with a wink, 'what are you doing with this loser?'

'I don't know . . . Chilling, I guess . . . timepass.'

'Yeah, timepass, man . . .' Dhruv agreed.

'Really? Have you seen your face? You look exactly like Kundan in *Raanjhanaa*!' said Karan. The Bollywood movie depicted an average-looking, dark-complexioned boy called Kundan, who was in love with his childhood friend, the fair and beautiful Zoya.

Kavya burst out laughing.

Encouraged, Karan continued. 'Wait, that's the perfect analogy! You're exactly like Kundan and Zoya, except that you, Dhruv, make Kundan look like a supermodel!'

'Get lost, dude!' said Dhruv, embarrassed. 'Isn't your auto waiting? You should leave now. Go!'

Kavya, who was thoroughly enjoying herself, piped up. 'I like this. I'm going to use this.'

Karan and Kavya burst out laughing while Dhruv managed a giggle. 'Thanks a lot, Karan. After all, what are old friends for?'

Then he added more seriously, 'Hey, why don't you come home? We'll all have a beer.'

Kavya nodded in agreement.

'No, man, I'll come next time for sure. I just had drinks and then stuffed myself at the hotel. I really should be heading back. Next time, definitely,' Karan refused politely, trying to keep his face impassive, but Dhruv caught on immediately.

'At the hotel, eh? So you are also giving tuitions.'

Karan turned to Kavya. 'It was such a pleasure meeting you! I'll see you guys later.'

'The next time you come, please let us know. We'll plan something and have a great time. It's been really long since we chilled out together,' Dhruv said, hugging Karan.

Karan walked towards the waiting autorickshaw.

'Do all Delhi boys sound the same?' Kavya mocked Dhruv.

Meanwhile, Karan, who had left, asked the autorickshaw to stop and came back to Dhruv and Kavya.

He pulled Dhruv aside. Though he was trying to be discreet, Kavya caught a few words and figured out what was being discussed.

'Go straight, take a right, and you will find a twenty-four-hour medical store there,' Dhruv explained.

It was a great chance for Kavya to get rid of the 'Fire and Ice' condoms, and she acted fast.

Without saying a word, she took the packet out and placed it in Karan's hand.

'Here, use it. It's our favourite.'

'Dude!' Dhruv was about to explain their idea of experimenting when he caught Kavya's eye and understood it was a prank. He nodded innocently.

'You're supercool, Kavya. In case you ever decide to leave this loser, please let me know. Give me a call. Dhruv has my number!' Karan joked. He was really impressed with Kavya.

'I'm getting late . . . and laid! So it's a great night for me. See you two soon!' he waved goodbye.

'Have fun!' Dhruv and Kavya spoke together, trying their best to hold back their smiles.

Kavya was feeling very smug.

'So proud of yourself, aren't you?' Dhruv pulled Kavya's cheeks.

'Very!' she said as they laughed and headed home.

3

'Kavvu, please come here and talk!' Dhruv yelled.

He was in the kitchen, making himself a sandwich. Kavya was talking to him from another room and he couldn't make sense of what she was saying.

Dhruv and Kavya had got back from the pharmacy but neither of them was sleepy. Kavya stomped into the kitchen, visibly upset. 'Why are you ignoring me?' She propped herself up on the kitchen counter.

'I'm not ignoring you, Kavvu. I just couldn't hear anything. Want a sandwich?'

'How can you be hungry again? We had such a heavy dinner and then we had ice cream too!'

'Yeah, but those ice creams fell down on the road because of that idiot Karan. And so I'm still hungry. I haven't eaten enough. Yes or no for the sandwich?'

Kavya gave in. 'Yeah, okay, make one for me as well.' She was feeling low and now she was going to stress-eat to feel better.

'Listen, Vivek's getting engaged,' she said with a pout.

'Vivek?' Dhruv tried to recall, and then grinned.

'Oh, Vivek! Your first boyfriend. The one from Nagpur! Isn't he the same guy who put up a photo collage of his mother and you on Facebook and captioned it "Lovers"?'

'That was in fifth grade, Dhruv! Will you stop remembering weird things about my exes?' Kavya was distressed and Dhruv wasn't helping.

'But it's funny, dude!'

'I'm serious.' Kavya turned her attention back to Facebook, checking the latest status update from her ex-boyfriend.

Dhruv could see that the more serious he got, the more it would affect Kavya. He tried to keep things light-hearted. 'Serious? Yeah, wait. We should take this seriously. Salami! We should use salami . . .' He moved towards the refrigerator.

'Do you want salami in your sandwich?'

'Yeah, okay, whatever,' she said, preoccupied. 'But it's so weird to know that he is getting engaged. He was my first boyfriend and the longest one.'

'Wow! So nice! Did you just say that?' Dhruv asked with a grin on his face. He was trying to hold back his laughter.

'I mean, that was the longest relationship that I was a part of. Stop being cheap!'

'What cheap? You said it! I'm just repeating it.'

'Won't you feel weird too if one of your exes got engaged or married?'

Dhruv took a minute before responding. With the knife in his hand, he gestured, 'It depends, you know. If the pretty one gets married, yes. But if the other one, the "blah" one gets married, then I'll be like, "Yeah whatever, she got married. Good for her!"'

'What! That's so Delhi-ish of you!'

'What's so Delhi-ish about this? If that other guy, that Nagpur part two, who used to call you what?—"*Jaanu*, jaanu"—if he gets married, would you really be upset? Be honest,' he said turning around and looking at her intently.

'First of all, he was my boyfriend in high school.'

'No, no . . . be honest.'

'Will you stop making me feel weird, please?' This wasn't how she had anticipated their conversation would go.

Dhruv placed his hands on her shoulders. 'I am not trying to make you feel anything, Kavya. All I'm saying is that it's good to remember the fun things about exes and forget the bad shit. How else will you date again?'

He smiled at her with so much warmth that she felt comforted. He made so much sense.

They left it at that and were soon enjoying their sandwiches while watching Aziz Ansari's show *Master of None*. Dhruv was laughing, but Kavya sat still, sombre and lost in thought. Dhruv had finished his sandwich, but Kavya was eating like a squirrel.

A really hilarious scene left Dhruv in splits. As he laughed, he realized that Kavya was not laughing with him.

'Did you see that?' he asked, looking at a sullen Kavya. She didn't seem interested.

'Are you still thinking about him?'

'Yes.' She nibbled at her sandwich. Then she threw up her hands in exasperation. 'I checked out that girl's profile. And she's pretty. Now I'm feeling even worse.'

Dhruv looked at her. Kavya was torturing herself over something insignificant, but it needed to be sorted out in her head, and he needed to help her do that. He switched off the TV and turned to face her, taking her hands in his.

'Okay, Kavvu, this is simple maths . . .'

Kavya groaned and slumped on the couch. Dhruv made her sit up straight. Kavya began whining.

'No, Momo, no maths. I really can't deal with that right now. It'll all go over my head.'

'No, no, listen . . . It's all going to make sense, I promise.'

Kavya looked carefully at Dhruv, asking him to go on.

'See, 97 per cent of Indian males who get married are between the age of eighteen and thirty-five. This means that according to the sex ratio, if you have 100 friends, fifty-two of them will be boys and forty-eight will be girls, obviously assuming that you show no bias towards any sex while making friends.'

Dhruv knew that understanding numbers was not Kavya's strong suit. So he took her plate, divided the chips into 'male' and 'female' and used them to explain the concept to her.

'Out of these fifty-two males, you must have dated at least three,' he continued. Kavya rolled her eyes.

Dhruv laughed at her exaggerated reaction. 'Just say yes. Don't act innocent.' Kavya smiled. Not only did Dhruv accept everything about her and her past, he also made sure that she felt no shame about the not-so-great bits of it.

'So the chances of your ex not getting married are . . .' He took one of the chips from the plate and took a huge bite of it so that only a crumb was left in his hand. He held it out to her and continued, '. . . only 0.03 per cent. It makes absolutely no difference.'

'What's your point, Momo?' Kavya asked, still unsure of what Dhruv was trying to say.

'The point is that him getting married is actually a normal thing. What you should do is send him a congratulatory message. And also warn him: "Please don't make another photo collage of your wife and mother and put it up as your display picture on Facebook. Because that shit isn't cool, man!"'

Kavya broke into a wry smile. 'That was a long time ago, Dhruv!'

Dhruv widened his eyes and dramatically replied, 'I'm just saying. He is capable of doing that. You know that. That's all I am saying.'

Kavya broke into a giggle. Even in the most tense of situations, Dhruv always managed to sort her mind out and make her laugh. She felt a lot better. The problem solved, she finally took the first proper bite from her sandwich.

'Send him a message and you'll feel better. And even if you don't, give it two days. You will forget about this. We're too busy to remember any of this for too long. You know that,' Dhruv said matter-of-factly.

It was true. Problems that seemed to have no solution, which felt like the end of the world, always faded and became insignificant with time. It was inevitable.

'Wow, what an amazing speech, Kundan!' Kavya teased.

'No! What has Karan taught you? Is this going to be your new thing?' He was happy to play along if it took Kavya's mind away from her issues.

'Hmm . . .' Kavya nodded, smiling mischievously. It was not going to be just her new thing. She was going to tell all his friends about it as well! However, she was still thinking about their discussion.

'Yeah, I guess you're right,' she said, turning serious. 'He is a nice guy. And I suppose I am happy for him.'

'How nice! Now can we finish the topic here? The mosquitoes in our room have died of old age, but we're still here, talking about the same thing.'

Kavya decided to change the subject and the mood.

'Momo, this sandwich is really good. One of your bests so far! Well done! I'd have asked you to consider being a chef, but there's no point because you'd eat everything you ever made.'

'Please leave the humour to me. I am the funny one in this relationship.' He then watched with sad, hungry eyes as Kavya took a bite of her sandwich.

She knew that look very well, but asked, 'What?'

'Bite? Please?'

'No.'

Dhruv pretended to be dejected. Kavya knew that there was no fighting it, that she

112

would give in because the sad expression on his face would beat her will.

'Okay, one small bite.' Her face showed that she had given in but was not happy about it.

'Small bite, remember. Please take only a small bite.'

Dhruv took the sandwich from her and helped himself to a huge bite right from the centre.

'Why would you do that!'

'Do what?' he asked innocently, relishing the big, juicy bit.

'I gave you my sandwich and you took a huge bite, that too right from the middle! That's the best part of the sandwich, Dhruv. This is horrible!' Kavya snatched her sandwich back and bit into it hungrily.

'See, these are the things you should be feeling bad about. Not your ex getting married. That shit doesn't matter.'

'Yeah, yeah. I get the point. But that was just you being a glutton. Don't try to make it look like

you did it to teach me a lesson. I'm still hungry.
Will you make another one and we split?'

Dhruv, who never shied away from food,
was as pleased as Punch. 'Now we're talking!
Give me two minutes, I'll make another one.
Then we'll get a good night's sleep.'

'What's the connection?'

'The more you eat, the better you sleep,' he
said, imparting another one of his Dhruvisms.
'Even pandas do that.'

'Pandas,' Kavya smiled, 'don't have to get
up and go to work in the morning.'

'They're damn lucky, come to think of it.'

'I can't believe we are having this
conversation. What time is it?'

'3.30 a.m.'

'3.30 a.m.!'

'Let's just finish this episode and sleep,'
Dhruv said pressing the play button once
again. Kavya moved closer to him and they
settled down cozily to watch. Soon they were
fast asleep, her slender body fitting perfectly
against his, oblivious to the lights and sounds
of the TV.

Good Night

Meanwhile, Dhruv's phone was buzzing with messages:

BC! G★★★u! What condom was it?
I started burning down there! Both me and the girl thought we had contracted some STD.
What kind of things are you guys into?
Fucker.

THANK YOU!

1

'Ughhh!' Kavya smacked her forehead in frustration as the autorickshaw driver told her that he had no change.

She was having another difficult start to the day and the week. First, there had been no warm water to bathe as the geyser had not been working. Kavya hated bathing in cold water even in the hot and humid weather of Mumbai because it gave her a jolt that she found extremely unpleasant.

Second, she was having a bad hair day. As she tried to comb her wild locks, one tuft just refused to settle down. No matter how much she brushed it, it popped right back up. She knew it was bothering her more than it should, but she just couldn't stop feeling conscious.

Looking angrily into the mirror she was reminded of Medusa, who had coiled snakes for hair. Legend had it that anyone who looked directly at Medusa turned to stone.

Nah, I'm way too pretty for that! Kavya told herself, waving away the cloud of dark thoughts. Her hair was super curly and she was just having a bad hair day, she counselled herself.

But her resolve to stay positive broke as every autorickshaw she flagged down refused to go to her destination. She had to wait for fifteen minutes in the hot Mumbai sun before she finally found one that agreed to take her to her office. By then, her hair had become even more frizzy and unmanageable. She was drenched in sweat and her face felt as if it had collected all the dust in the world.

And now the autorickshaw driver didn't have change. She would have to take an extra two-minute ride to the vada pav stall, earnestly request the vendor, plead with him even, for change for a hundred bucks, then head back and probably be late for work—again!

Mondays, I hate you! she thought as she stepped into her office complex. She thought about how one spent two days of the weekend doing exactly what one wanted—sleeping in late, waking up late, eating what one wanted—only to face the Monday bomb!

'I haven't even eaten anything since morning!' Kavya grumbled as she stepped into her office. Immediately, she was gripped by the aroma of hot, spicy food. She picked up pace so she could drop her bag at the desk and then chase the heavenly fragrance, no matter where it took her.

She reached her desk a few seconds later and found Kirtana pacing up and down restlessly.

'Where have you been? I was waiting for you! I'm so hungry that I'm getting a headache. And this smell is driving me nuts. Come on!' She grabbed Kavya's arm and pulled her across the office.

'Aww, you're such a great friend!' Kavya pulled Kirtana into an awkward hug while walking towards the conference room, from where the aroma seemed to be coming.

They entered the conference room to find a lavish, sumptuous spread waiting for them. Many of their colleagues were already serving themselves and many were halfway through.

'Vipul had his first baby, a girl. And he's treating the whole office to authentic Hyderabadi food!' Kirtana whispered into Kavya's ear, knowing very well that she would be so caught up with the food that she would forget to congratulate Vipul.

Kavya's eyes widened at the array of dishes in front of her: *boti* kebab, chicken tikka, *payaa*, korma and, not to forget, her favourite— biryani! She moved forward, almost as if in a trance, and found Vipul standing with a grin on his face.

'Congratulations, Vipul! I'm so happy for you! You turned out to be the Santa Claus of this office. I hope you keep having kids and treating us to amazing food!'

Vipul laughed and asked her to enjoy the meal.

Kavya helped herself to everything and dipped her fork into the chicken tikka. She took a bite, closed her eyes and let the flavours explode in her mouth. The meat was so tender and succulent; she could taste every ingredient. 'Mmm . . .' she moaned in ecstasy. The fact that she had not had breakfast made this meal all the more rewarding.

Suddenly, her food haze was interrupted by the buzzing of her phone in her hand.

There were a series of messages—more like reminders—from Dhruv.

Dhruv
Online

Kavu don't forget that we're going to that Iranian cafe tonight.

So please have a light lunch and get done on time. Today is Mutton Cutlet day.

Yay! Say shava shava mahiya say mutton cutlet soniya!

The moment Kavya read the message, her heart sank. It was a conundrum: should she leave this mouth-watering food for dinner at the Iranian cafe, or should she have what was available to her right here, right now? The bird in hand was so much more tempting than the two in the bush in the future.

She tried to resist as much as she could, but eventually it wasn't her decision to make.

She was just following the biryani. The scent enticed her, enchanted her, and cast its spell over her.

'To hell with it!' She gave in, helped herself to a huge serving and greedily stuffed spoonfuls into her mouth. There was no stopping her. Naturally, she was overcome with guilt once she finished. Dhruv had been planning this date for weeks and they had finally managed to fix it for today. His disappointed face flashed before her eyes.

I won't tell him about it! she thought as she returned to her desk.

2

'Where are you?' Dhruv asked Kavya on the phone.

He had taken a cab and come to Kavya's office to pick her up. And now he was waiting— mutton cutlets the only thing on his mind as he tapped his feet impatiently.

'I'm in a meeting, Dhruv.'

'What meeting? What is this, Kavvu?' Dhruv's excitement dropped several notches. 'Okay, wrap up quickly. I'm starving.'

'I'm waiting downstairs,' he added, but she had already disconnected the call.

Just then his mobile phone beeped.

Sorry! I couldn't help it. It's not my fault. 🙏

The meeting was called at the last moment.

Help! Save me! 🙌

Dhruv typed out:

This is not done, yaar, Kavvu.

You could have told them in the morning that you needed to leave early.

His phone beeped again.

Don't worry, Momo.

We'll be there on time.

I won't be long.

Sit tight!

He replied:

Come fast. I'm starving.

I am waiting right under your office.

Hoping that it would be a short wait, Dhruv plugged in his headphones. He rested his head against the cab window and watched silently as

125

the world passed him by. He kept peeking at the driver to see if he was getting impatient and could see him get more and more fidgety and restless.

After about ten minutes of waiting, the driver turned around. He didn't speak, but looked at Dhruv with an expression that said it all. Dhruv knew this was bound to happen, he was waiting for the inevitable. It was not the driver's fault.

'Sorry.' He slowly stepped out of the cab and paid the driver. Now he didn't even have a place to sit.

In the distance he saw a tiny tea stall and decided to have some chai while he waited for Kavya. As he sipped the chai, he spotted another stall selling chaat. His stomach immediately began growling—he hadn't eaten anything in a while now, and he had a penchant for street food. But he had set his mind on having mutton cutlets for dinner and nothing was going to distract him from that.

You shouldn't waste your appetite on street food. You've been waiting to eat those cutlets for so long now and you're travelling so far for them. You can have chaat any day! Dhruv fought against the temptation.

He began looking for something to do to take his attention away from the chaat. He pulled out his mobile phone and started going through his Facebook feed, but soon got bored and switched to Instagram. After scrolling for thirty seconds, his restlessness began catching up with him. He called his mother, but she was busy visiting a relative.

'What is this, yaar!' Dhruv yelled in frustration and kicked a stone on the footpath. 'It's always something or the other!' he grumbled as all past instances of Kavya getting him late came back to him. 'Why doesn't she understand that the cafe will shut down?'

Dhruv was pacing up and down the sidewalk, animatedly having a conversation with himself. People around him thought that he was crazy. Just as he was about to give up, Kavya called. Dhruv answered immediately.

'Sorry, sorry, sorry, Momo!'

Dhruv couldn't say much. 'How much longer yaar, Kavvu?'

'I'm just taking the lift and coming down. You're still downstairs, right?'

'Yes, come fast.' He cut the call and booked another cab on his mobile phone.

As Kavya stepped out of the building, she saw Dhruv having a very animated conversation on the phone. She crossed the road and walked towards him. As she approached him, she caught parts of the conversation.

'Why can't you just follow the directions and come to the location? I am standing exactly there!' Dhruv was talking to the cab driver.

'Where is the cab? I thought you were waiting for me in one.'

Dhruv hadn't spotted Kavya coming. 'The cab left! Why would it wait so long?'

He got back to his phone. 'Yes, come straight down that road. No, you don't have to take a turn, just keep coming straight!'

Clearly, the cab driver was getting on his nerves. 'Why can't he just come to the location I had sent? Or better still, just stop and ask someone for directions. It's so much easier that way. How can I guide him standing here?'

Dhruv was very agitated. It was unlike him—he was generally calm, composed and always knew what to do. Kavya stood on the side and looked at him. The pressure of reaching the cafe on time so he would not miss out on those mutton cutlets was really getting to him.

'You're at Mohan Medical? How would I know where Mohan Medical is? Why don't you stop for a second and ask someone for directions?' Dhruv turned around to see Kavya laughing.

'Why are you laughing, Kavya? This is really annoying!'

But Kavya could not help it. Dhruv got even more flustered when she took out her mobile phone and began recording a video of him trying not to lash out at the driver and telling him where to reach. She brought the phone closer to him as he talked. He swatted her arm away.

'Get that phone out of my face, Kavya! . . . What? You've reached some temple? Where did you find a temple here? Oh my God, where have you reached?' Dhruv was on the edge, just a step away from calling it quits, canning the whole plan, going home, passing out and just putting this day behind him.

'Dhruv, you idiot, there is a temple here! Look, it's there!' Kavya pointed into the distance. And just like that, the crisis came to an end. Dhruv got back on his phone and told the driver not to move an inch from where he was.

'Kavvu, please let's just walk to the temple. If I give him any more instructions, I don't know where he'll end up. I really don't know if this place will be open or not. Seriously, let's go!' He pulled Kavya along.

Once in the cab, Dhruv took a deep breath and calmed down. Then he looked at Kavya who was panting because of all the walking and jogging. He smiled and put his arm around her shoulder. 'How was your day, Kavvu?'

The driver turned the keys, the engine roared and the two of them took off on their gastronomic adventure!

3

As their cab turned the last corner to the cafe, Dhruv's heart started beating really fast. He was almost sweating with anticipation. They were stuck at a signal and Dhruv just could not bear the tension any more. He stuck his head out of the window, strained his neck as much as he could and tried to see if the cafe was open.

It was, but there weren't many people in there. They were probably taking their last orders. Dhruv panicked and asked the driver to end the trip. There was no point asking him to take a U-turn to the other side of the road. Then, taking Kavya's hand, Dhruv literally ran across the road. He hesitated outside the cafe, wondering if it had closed for the day. But when no one stopped him from entering, he heaved a sigh of relief.

'Yes! I will eat mutton cutlets today!'

Kavya laughed.

Their happiness did not last long though.

They settled down at a comfortable table on the side from where they could see the chaos on the road outside and also soak in the cozy ambience of the quiet, worn-out cafe.

'Thank God we made it, Kavvu. I would have been really upset if this place had been shut.'

'I told you this place would be open! Loser, you got mad at me for no reason.' Kavya felt happy for Dhruv.

As the waiter approached them with the menu card, Dhruv's excitement began building up again. There was something that the prospect of having food did to him that nothing else could—not even the prospect of sex.

'No need for the menu. Just get us two portions of mutton cutlet gravy, please.'

At first Kavya thought that there was no reason to get Dhruv agitated, and that no matter how full she was she'd just have something with him. But with all the Hyderabadi food already in her stomach she had to interrupt him. 'No, just get one.'

Dhruv gave her a puzzled look.

'We'll share?'

Dhruv gave her a look of shock and horror. 'I don't want to share!' Then he asked the waiter to get the cutlets with bread on the side.

'There are no mutton cutlets left,' said the waiter matter-of-factly. 'That was the last one.' He looked at a table behind them.

Dhruv turned to see a couple thoroughly enjoying the cutlets. 'What the hell!'

People seated at the other tables immediately turned towards them.

'Shhh . . . It's okay, Momo. Relax!' Kavya was a little embarrassed.

Dhruv took a deep breath. 'Sorry, bro, but can you please check in your kitchen once again? I'm sure you'll find one piece at least.' There was a part of Dhruv that couldn't believe that life had cheated him of food. After all this effort, he deserved the cutlets.

133

'I've checked, and it's not there,' came the crisp reply. The waiter was clearly getting impatient. It was almost closing time and he was stuck with two guests who were making the last part of his tiring day even more strenuous.

Kavya wished that he'd just go in and then tell them that it was over instead of saying it like that. 'Please go in and check?' Kavya requested.

'Yes, please. We have come from really far just for your mutton cutlets. Please just check.' Dhruv was desperate.

By then the waiter had had enough. He turned to the two of them. 'Madam, Sir. I'm telling you this after checking. Why would I lie to you? Now if you want something else, let me know, else I'm leaving.' He had one of those faces that never showed emotion, the kind that never smiled, the kind that was always grumpy and wore a grim, rigid expression throughout the day.

'Okay, get us two mutton biryanis . . .' Dhruv began.

'No, just one,' Kavya interrupted.

'Why?'

'I won't be able to finish it and it'll go to waste.'

'I can't believe this, man!' Dhruv was having a bad day and was taking every single thing the wrong way. The weight of it all was bogging him down. 'Okay, just get us one plate.'

'Two or one?' asked the irritated waiter.

Kavya could see all the effort it was taking for Dhruv to not fly off the handle. She decided to step in.

'Just one!' She gestured for the waiter to leave.

'What the hell, Kavya? Why are you not eating? Are you feeling unwell? This is biryani we are talking about.'

Kavya knew she couldn't keep the truth from him for long. So she decided to just confess.

'Honestly, I forgot about this and somebody in office got really amazing Hyderabadi food for everyone. And I ate too much of it!'

This upset Dhruv even more. 'What? Seriously? I haven't eaten anything since afternoon. I only had biscuits so that I could come and enjoy this meal with you. I was really looking forward to this, Kavya . . . This is not done! And then you got me late. I thought I'd come here and have mutton cutlet gravy . . .'

'The biryani is also over.' The grumpy server returned and cut Dhruv off.

By now, Dhruv had had it. He slapped his forehead and buried his face in his arms. It just wasn't his day!

'You should have come earlier. Everything is over by this hour.' The waiter added insult to injury.

'Okay, just get us the best thing that you have available right now.' Kavya tried to get rid of him so that he didn't agitate Dhruv any more.

'All we have left is scrambled eggs with bread.'

'Just get a two-egg scramble with bread.'

'Wow!' Dhruv rolled his eyes. 'So I came all the way and travelled for two hours to have scrambled eggs? I could've got this at the street vendor close to our apartment as well.'

Dhruv's anger was flying out like sparks. He gave Kavya an accusing look, which set her off as well.

'What! It's not my fault that they ran out of food!'

'We should not have come today!' Dhruv was angry. 'First, you forgot. Then, you ate your fill and came. This is a dinner date, Kavya. What was the point of coming today if you weren't going to eat?'

'I came for you! Because you were so excited about it.' Kavya could not understand why Dhruv didn't appreciate her intent.

'What is this formality? You don't have to come anywhere for me. What's the point of this if it's just going to annoy both of us?' Dhruv was equally caustic.

They were both talking, but the problem was that neither was listening. They even argued about how many eggs they wanted scrambled. That's when Kavya realized that Dhruv was getting so irritated because he was hungry. He had been looking forward to this and had barely eaten the whole day. Once Kavya was clear about that, she knew what she had to do—wait for Dhruv to eat. Her tone became friendlier and gentler.

'What formality, Momo? Chill. We came here because you wanted to. And we're here now.'

The waiter got the food, placed it in front of them without a word and left, which was a good thing because Dhruv did not need any more riling up.

'Yeah.' Dhruv's volume dropped a few notches. 'Let's just not talk right now. Let me enjoy my scrambled eggs in peace.' He did not want the fight to escalate any more. He sullenly tore a piece of bread, stuffed some egg into it, put it into his mouth and began chewing. As soon as his tongue embraced the flavour and the aroma caressed his nose, he felt better. Before he knew it, he had polished off the whole plate.

Kavya smiled. It was at times like these that she knew she loved to be with Dhruv. They had developed a comfortable bond. Once she had had her fill of watching Dhruv savour his meal, Kavya took a tissue and began sketching—an old habit.

The cafe was old and the building that housed it was rickety. However, the character of the place was unmistakable in its walls, furniture and crockery. The ambience contained so much history that once Kavya began sketching, she was fully absorbed. Sitting there was like travelling back in time. There were so many picturesque frames in the cafe to capture. Kavya couldn't help but sketch and take back a piece of this quaint cafe.

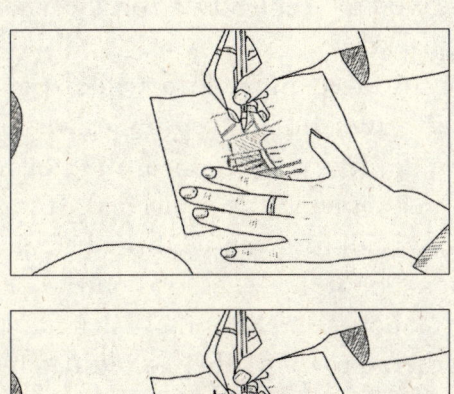

The cafe was empty by the time Dhruv finished eating. It was closing time. The waiter was waiting for Dhruv to finish. As soon as he put the last bite in his mouth, before he even got a chance to chew, the waiter walked up to them and placed the bill on the table.

Dhruv reached into his pocket for his wallet, but Kavya grabbed the bill. 'It's on me!'

Dhruv couldn't help but smile. 'Why? Because you're feeling bad for me and my dinner plans?'

Kavya looked up at him while trying to find her wallet in her bag and gave him a small smile. It was true, but it did not really matter, no apologies were needed. It was all good, it was all forgiven—Dhruv had already forgotten about it. That was what was so amazing about the love they shared. They were tethered to each other so intimately that they never lost sight of the other and their love. They could be angry, annoyed or sad, but never in their hearts did they think ill or less of each other.

Dhruv broke out into his mischievous grin, the one that Kavya adored. 'In that case, can you please add caramel custard to the bill as well?'

The waiter said matter-of-factly, 'Not available', picked up the money and the bill and walked away. Now that Dhruv wasn't hungry, he found it funny. Both of them burst out laughing.

As they walked out, Dhruv took Kavya's hand in his and they walked in silence. Their eyes met for a brief moment and both of them broke into genuine, beaming smiles. It had been over two years since they had begun dating, but the romance hadn't died. And that was the most heartening, and the most comforting, thought for both of them.

Young love might have its charm—it is exciting, exhilarating and intoxicating, but it doesn't hold a candle to old, knowing, comforting love. As Dhruv and Kavya strolled down the old streets of Mumbai, their young love too aged a bit.

4

'Taxi!' Dhruv shouted for the nth time as another one passed them by without stopping. They had been looking for a cab for over twenty minutes and both of them were losing patience. They were unable to book cabs on their phones as those were running at exorbitant surge prices.

Suddenly, and much to their surprise, they saw a cab go ahead and then stop for them. They were so glad that they ran to it, opened the door, and jumped in.

'Finally!'

They thanked the driver for stopping.

'Sorry, I didn't see you there.'

A courteous and polite cab driver!

'Please take us to Powai,' Dhruv said.

'Why? Aren't we going to Bandra?'

The driver was about to start the engine, but stopped after Kavya's question.

'What? Why?'

'It's Taboo night at Shifa's! Don't tell me you forgot!'

'What! That's today?' Dhruv realized that there was more to the day.

'No.' He protested. 'I'm not going! I just want to go home and watch the new episode of *Game of Thrones*! I downloaded it and haven't even seen a single scene. You know how difficult that is for me? I even bought popcorn!'

Dhruv was pushing with all his might to not go. This was not how he had planned the rest of the evening.

'We can watch that tomorrow too, no, Dhruv?'

'No, someone will ruin the episode for me with a spoiler. It's a party, someone will surely talk about it. Let's not go. And wait, don't you want to watch the episode? Or have you already seen that too, like you already ate today?'

'Shut up, Dhruv, stop being so difficult. We decided five days ago that we'd go for Shifa's Taboo night. And I am also wearing my new earrings. You're the one who keeps saying that I ignore my friends for us.'

'Kavya, my head does not work like that. I don't maintain a calendar. And who keeps a party on a Monday night anyway?'

'You know it's her thing, Dhruv. We missed the last four Taboo nights. Let's not miss this one. We'll leave early?' Kavya tried her best to convince him.

'That never happens. No one in the history of parties has ever said "we'll leave early" and then actually done that. Don't just say it because you want to go.'

The cab driver, who was watching them argue, waited a while to let them make up their minds. He was already regretting stopping for them. Holding his head in his hands, he cursed his luck. All he wanted to do was to earn some money, go home, eat and sleep. He had enough problems of his own and didn't have time for all this bickering.

'If all you want to do is fight, then please get out of my cab.'

Dhruv and Kavya got out of the cab, slammed the doors shut and started squabbling. Again. One moment they had felt intense, immense love, and the next moment they were fighting in the middle of a road. It was like they were continuously being tossed from one end of a tennis court to another, with the cab driver sitting outside, his head moving from Kavya to Dhruv and back.

'Can't you just go alone? Do I have to come?'

'Really, Dhruv? Are you really asking me to go alone? Did I not come to eat with you at this place?'

'Wait. That's why you came? Because you wanted me to go to Shifa's party?'

The driver had had enough. He blew the horn asking both of them to move away from the cab. Once they did, he sped away.

'You're really being an idiot, Dhruv. I can't believe you're asking me to go alone. Have some shame!'

'Shame? Don't talk to me like my mother, Kavya. Why would you say "Did I not come to eat with you?" Is this an exchange offer?'

Kavya couldn't believe that Dhruv was thinking these things, let alone saying them. Did he think so little of her?

Her reply was cold. 'To make you realize that I'd happily do anything for you and that I expect you to do the same for me.'

Dhruv knew she was right and that he was being difficult. When Kavya talked about happily doing things for him, he couldn't hit back. He softened immediately. 'Arre, don't say emotional stuff like this. It just messes with my head and I keep changing my mind.'

This did nothing to calm Kavya down. She looked away and didn't say anything. When the silence got too much, too awkward for Dhruv, he asked, 'So . . . like . . . what? Can you go alone?'

Kavya wanted to shout at him and curse him. It took every ounce of her strength to not do that. He seemed to be testing her repeatedly and she knew there was no point continuing the conversation. She took a deep breath and walked away.

Dhruv stood rooted to the spot. He knew she was right. But he also knew that he did not want to go. What a rollercoaster this day was turning out to be!

5

Loud music, chaos, laughs and shrieks. They could hear the party from outside Shifa's apartment block. It was exactly what Dhruv was not in the mood for, everything that he was dreading!

After their fight, neither had said a word throughout the forty-five-minute ride to Shifa's place. After they got off the cab, Dhruv wanted to run home, but he stuck around. He might have dragged his feet every step of the way, but he never stopped following Kavya. No matter how much he did not want to go, he'd never leave her alone.

They entered the elevator, still silent. Their eyes met briefly for a second, but both of them quickly looked away. This was getting too much for Dhruv to take. He desperately wanted to put up one more argument, use his last straw of resistance before they entered Shifa's home. So the moment Kavya reached for the doorbell, Dhruv broke his silence. 'Listen, Kavvu, there's still time. Think about it, we can still get out of here.'

Kavya paused midway. With her hand still in the air, she turned and gave Dhruv a cold stare.

'Fuck you.' She spoke through clenched teeth. She didn't shout at him. That would have been okay. What made these two words sound like an ultimatum was the coldness and calmness with which they had been spoken. Dhruv understood that it meant the end of their argument, but he decided to be grumpy anyway.

Soon the door was flung open by a girl with a pixie haircut. She was wearing an elegant, salmon-coloured off-shoulder top and a little black skirt. Kavya's face stretched into a huge smile as soon as she saw her friend. They screamed each other's name excitedly.

'Shifaaaaa!'

'Kavyaaa!'

They had once been roommates and best friends in college. But now they didn't meet as often as they would have liked to. But whenever they did, it was like they were back in college,

148

in that same messy room they had called home for three years.

They hugged while Dhruv waited awkwardly. Dhruv was a little taken aback by how quickly Kavya's mood had changed. Soon Adi, Shifa's boyfriend, came and greeted him.

'Hey, Dhruv is also here!' he announced with a wide grin. 'So good to see you, man. You're never here. Such a nice, pleasant surprise!'

Dhruv refused to smile but thanked him as he shook his hand and entered the house. 'Nice house!' he complimented Shifa and Adi. Then he headed straight to the couch and sat all by himself.

Being the social person that she was, Kavya started mingling with everyone. Someone had come up with a brilliant idea of putting a karaoke machine in the midst of some very drunk people. Every now and then there would come a burst of bad singing that would make Dhruv cringe. Some of his favourite songs were being ruined forever. The fact that he was sober made it more torturous.

Someone offered Dhruv a joint and then some beer, both of which he politely refused. He was going to stick to his tonic water that day. *How the hell were people getting so drunk and high on a Monday? They were all going to repent this the next morning*, he thought grumpily.

There was a time when Dhruv could have done the same—stayed up late and gone to office with a hangover. He was younger and had just started working. But that seemed like decades ago. The present-day Dhruv only drank on weekends and special days, that too extremely cautiously.

As he sat by himself, he watched people talk, eat, drink and enjoy themselves. Instinctively, he looked around for Kavya. He noticed her talking to someone in a red T-shirt. She seemed to be highly amused by him and was laughing uncontrollably at his jokes.

Dhruv's mind was immediately on high alert. As he watched them laugh and smile, insecurity raised its ugly head. *What are they talking about? Why does she look so happy? Who is he?*

After a few minutes, the same guy came and sat beside Dhruv and began talking to him. Dhruv realized that he was drunk and babbling away. The only thing he did manage to catch was his name: Rahul.

Dhruv decided that he too would chill out, loosen up and stop being so rigid. He sat more comfortably on the sofa and grabbed a beer. That was when he noticed Kavya looking worriedly towards Rahul and him. She looked tense for some reason.

Then Adi came into the room and his eyes fell on Rahul and Dhruv. He found a way to shoo Rahul away and began talking to Dhruv. For a while, Dhruv was distracted and forgot about Kavya. For a while, he genuinely relaxed and chatted without a care in the world. Then his thoughts automatically turned towards Kavya and he looked around for her. He couldn't spot her. His eyes darted around the room, but she was nowhere to be seen.

He excused himself and decided to look in the adjoining rooms. As soon as he opened the door to the first room, he heard the soundtrack of *Game of Thrones* and saw five people huddled in front of a laptop. 'Get out!'

Dhruv did not need to be told twice. He slammed the door behind him. He was determined to not let any spoilers ruin his experience of the series.

When he entered the second room, he was taken aback. A guy and girl, drunk beyond words, were trying to put their clothes back on. 'Shit! Sorry!' Dhruv was embarrassed and quickly shut the door.

What the hell is happening at this party? Dhruv thought to himself. He decided to go to the kitchen and check if Kavya was trying to sneak in a late bite. But secretly he just wanted to find something to eat for himself because nothing comforted him like food. It was like a small break from the world—a temporary relief, a brief respite from the weight on his chest.

He entered the kitchen to find a man with really long dreadlocks, stoned out of his mind, chomping on a burger like his life depended on it. Had Dhruv not known that he was stoned, he'd have thought the man had not eaten in days.

His spirits immediately lifted at the thought of more food. He smiled at the guy. 'Hey, is there more?'

The guy stopped eating for a second and looked at his burger. 'No, I don't think so.' He then took the burger that he had more mutilated than eaten and offered it to Dhruv. 'This is the last one. Have it, bro.'

Dhruv felt his insides churn just looking at the burger, but he backed out. 'No, bro, you look really hungry. You have it. It's okay.'

By now, Dhruv was done with this looking-for-Kavya business. He did not want to open any more doors and witness things that made him want to gouge his eyes out. He took out his mobile phone to call her when he saw a Facebook notification from her. Kavya had posted a meme on his wall.

In a moment, all the load that was weighing him down and suffocating him was lifted. A sudden rush of happiness and love took over him and he couldn't help laughing. He was reminded of all the good times he'd had with her. All the happy memories that his bad mood had repressed came back to him. The cloud of doubt and anger was lifted.

He called her up, laughing. 'Where are you?'

'Balcony.'

In a jiffy, he was off to be with her.

As he went past the hall, he saw two people arguing about what to sing next for the karaoke.

Dhruv stopped. 'What about "Sing" by Travis?' It was one of Kavya's favourites and Dhruv wanted it to be playing when he saw her in the balcony after their tiff. It was one of those several small gestures that they made for each other.

As the song started playing, Dhruv saw Kavya's silhouette moving to the music in the balcony. She had his back towards him, which allowed him to use the oldest trick in the book. He tapped her on one shoulder and then darted to the opposite side. Expecting Dhruv to be right there, she turned and spoke excitedly. 'They're playing my favourite song!'

Though he intended to hide behind her for longer, simply to bug her a little more, he could not help himself. He wrapped his arms around her.

'You are so cute, Kavya.'

She laughed as they moved to the music together.

Once the music died down, Dhruv remembered why he had been looking for her. He pulled out his mobile phone and showed her the meme she had posted.

'What is all this, Kavvu?'

She pulled a mock-sad expression. 'What's wrong with that? We're not friends any more, right? Clearly, mutton cutlets are more important to you than me. You have been angry for so long now.'

'That's not true, love. You know that.' He ran his fingers through her hair. Then, trying to sound sexy, he said, 'You know I have eyes only for you . . .' His hands ran all over Kavya. She laughed and pushed him away as he tried to hold on to her.

'What was that guy in the red T-shirt telling you?' she asked.

'Nothing, yaar. I think he was stoned. Every two minutes he kept saying, "I'm Rahul . . . Hi, I'm Rahul . . . My name is Rahul . . ."'

Kavya heaved a sigh of relief. 'Thank God! I thought he was giving you *Game of Thrones* spoilers!'

'Wait, what? Is that what he was telling you?'

'Yeah, it's so irritating. I made it clear to him to stay away from you. And then I saw him talking to you and I thought he would tell you about the whole episode and ruin your mood. That meme was to cheer you up.'

'That's really, really messed up. How do such people even exist?' Dhruv understood the enormity of what could have happened.

'Chill na, Momo. I'm just glad it was me he gave the spoilers to and not you. I know how much it would have killed your mood.'

Just then, the five people who had been watching *Game of Thrones* in the other room came out to the balcony. They stood near Kavya and Dhruv, talking excitedly about the new episode. 'What a mad episode, yaar! I can't believe that . . .'

Before he could hear anything else, Dhruv covered his ears and ran inside, babbling to himself. Kavya ran behind him, giggling uncontrollably. The universe was clearly conspiring against Dhruv!

Dhruv got himself another beer. He felt much better, much lighter now that he wasn't angry any more, now that his emotions weren't overburdening him. He was loosening up, and just in time. They joined the others for a game of Taboo.

Taboo is played with cards. The goal is to get your teammates to guess the word you are describing, but there's a list of words you can't use while doing so. Also, there is a time limit within which the team members have to guess the word.

Shifa was cheered on as she brought the board game to the table. Teams were formed and Dhruv and Kavya ended up on opposite sides.

As the game progressed, one thing was for sure: Dhruv was on a roll! He was able to guess words without much prompting. Though Kavya was on the opposite team, she was extremely happy that Dhruv was on a winning streak. She was glad that he was finally involved and happy.

All was going great, and though some people had got very drunk and passed out, the rest of them were having fun. Then Adi threw a spanner in the works. He cheated. And he got caught immediately by Shifa.

'Thanks for spoiling my evening, Adi!' She stopped the game and stormed out of the room. There was an uncomfortable silence as everyone waited, wondering what to do.

Kavya and Adi went to Shifa's room to console her. As Dhruv sat waiting and sipped his beer, guests started leaving. Many of them, however, had passed out around him.

Then he saw Kavya talk to Adi and walk towards him. 'He said he cheated because he didn't want to look stupid in front of Shifa's friends.'

'That's sad.'

'I know. But he's always awkward around Shifa.' Kavya sat next to Dhruv and put his arm around her shoulders.

Both Dhruv and Kavya knew how lucky they were to be so comfortable with each other. They sat quietly for a while as Kavya played with her hair and Dhruv enjoyed his beer with his arm around her. When Kavya looked up, she saw Dhruv looking at the people left in the hall.

'What are you thinking about, Dhruv?'

'Hmm?' He took his time to answer. He was debating with himself whether he should have a chat about relationships or to let it go and lighten up. He decided to let it go.

'I was just looking around to see who here I'd like to sleep with.'

'How cheap!'

'What? I'm being honest. I could have come up with some deep, intellectual shit and got away with it, no? But I chose to be truthful.'

'Fair enough.' Kavya decided to play along. 'Even I'll check someone out now.'

'Is that right?'

'Of course! Do you think you alone can get away with it?

Both of them began looking at the people around.

'Who are you checking out?' Kavya looked in the same direction as Dhruv.

'See that girl in the blue skirt? She's pretty!'

160

That was as much as Kavya could take. She took one of the cushions on the couch and smacked Dhruv straight on the face with it.

'Ouch!' He laughed. They decided it was time to leave.

The elevator seemed like the perfect place to make out. As Kavya moved closer to Dhruv and the doors closed, they stole a kiss. They moved away when another couple entered the lift on the next floor.

The couple started talking. 'What an episode, man! How could they let Hodor die?'

Dhruv was shocked. The spoiler had been delivered, and how!

'What the hell!' Dhruv was frustrated. 'I told you this was going to happen at the party!'

'I'm sorry . . .' Kavya rubbed his shoulder to comfort him. 'But it didn't happen at the party, did it?' Dhruv, however, was inconsolable. He could never have imagined this was how it would end. The couple looked sheepishly at Dhruv and Kavya as if they had committed a

161

crime. They quickly walked out of the elevator as soon as it opened on the ground floor.

'Wait, I'll just call for a cab.' Kavya pulled out her mobile phone. Luckily, the taxi was just a minute away. But they weren't going back home. Oh no, Kavya was not going to let such a good day end on a bad note.

The night wasn't done. A surprise awaited Dhruv.

* * *

'How the hell did you even find this place?' Dhruv was puzzled.

This was one of the things that made Mumbai so special. They were sitting in a cafe at 1 a.m., waiting for their chicken shawarma rolls to arrive. And it wasn't even that they were alone or the city was quiet—there were people and traffic all around.

'After you got the spoiler in the elevator, I knew I had to cheer you up somehow. I did not want you to go to bed annoyed. And I know there's nothing that helps your mood like food. So, before booking a cab, I searched online for a place to eat.'

As she spoke, the waiter placed the rolls in front of them.

Dhruv looked dotingly at Kavya. It was so beautiful, the way she cared for him. He smiled widely. 'Am I really that easy to please?'

'Why are you worrying about it? It's a good thing, Momo.'

Dhruv picked up both the rolls in one go.

'Hello! One of them is for me!'

'But I thought you were not hungry?'

'Oh my God, Dhruv! I ate eight hours ago. How long are you going to hold that against me?'

'I was kidding!' He passed one roll to her.

Kavya watched him sink his teeth greedily into the roll. 'Listen, I'm sorry for today. I didn't mean to ruin your day.'

'Not an issue, it's not your fault.' And then he added, 'And anyway, I actually had fun at the party.'

'You did? You created such a fuss before going!'

'Fussing about it was justified back then. It's just that sometimes you would want to do something, and sometimes I would like to do something else. But as long as both of us are having fun, it's fine, no?' he asked.

'Yeah, that's true.'

'And everything can't be planned, right?'

'Exactly! Like, while coming in the cab, I saw a fair just a short walk away. So after we're done eating, I'm taking you there!'

Her excitement was so infectious that Dhruv was in a hurry to finish the roll and head to the fair. They wolfed down the shawarma rolls and walked away hand-in-hand. On the way, Dhruv tenderly kissed Kavya's hand. He kept wondering what good he had done to deserve someone as caring and thoughtful as her, especially when small things got him so worked up.

As they got closer to the fair, they could see the lights and hear the music. Their excitement grew. The fair was like entering a different dimension altogether. The sound of traffic and people outside had been muffled and replaced by repetitive techno music. All around them were a million colours and lights.

They bought cotton candy, blew soap bubbles in the air and sat on a carousel ride till Kavya's frizzy hair went so wild that it covered her face. Several other rides and games followed till they finally came to the one they had been saving for the end: the giant Ferris wheel.

It was huge! Their capsule reached the highest point and both of them looked down in awe. The wind caressed their faces, leaving Kavya's hair fluttering, even as the music below faded and gave them a moment of peace and silence. For miles around there were no tall buildings. They could see the silhouette of the hills far, far away and some of the farthest edges of Mumbai. They laughed and kissed.

This had been one of the best decisions they had taken, the best, most romantic night they had had in a long time, all thanks to Kavya. Left to himself, Dhruv would never have thought of coming to a fair in the middle of the night.

But they had each other, and where one lacked, the other made up. Kavya was the spontaneous and energetic half of the relationship while Dhruv was the more practical and passive half.

But even if given a choice, both of them would change nothing about the other.

HERE WE GO!

1

It was the earliest part of the day—the wee hours between dawn and sunrise—but Dhruv was bustling about the house like a man on a mission. Kavya was fast asleep, cozy under her quilt, blissfully oblivious to the commotion in the house. She was in the deepest, most peaceful phase of sleep when Dhruv's urgent voice rang through the house: 'Kavvu, please get up and close the door!'

'Hmm . . .' Kavya turned over in her sleep.

Dhruv called out again. 'Kavya, please come and close the door, I have to leave!' He waited for ten seconds, then walked into the room, kissed her on the cheek and shook her gently. 'Kavvu, I have to eat the bhajis today. Please get up.'

'All right. You wear your shoes and I'll be up, but you come here first.' She patted her bedside.

But Dhruv was in no mood to delay his plans. He walked out of the room and didn't return to give her another kiss. In fact, when she finally woke up, she couldn't hear him. It took her groggy brain almost a minute to register his absence. When it did, her eyes popped open. She threw the quilt aside, sprung out of bed and ran towards the hall, praying Dhruv hadn't left. She'd feel terrible if he had. Sunday was the only day they actually got to spend together—it was their day.

As she rushed into the drawing room, she heaved a sigh of relief as she saw Dhruv sitting on the couch, tying his shoelaces. Her face broke into the widest of smiles. For some reason, Dhruv knew that she would not let him go alone.

In his previous six attempts to have the bhajis, this temptation of cuddling with Kavya had proven to be the deal breaker. It was nicer to just hold her and go back to sleep. He knew that if he did not leave soon, there was a high chance of Kavya convincing him to come back to bed.

A friend and he had been travelling from Pune to Mumbai when they had got caught in a terrible traffic jam. They hadn't eaten for hours, which is why they had decided to take a detour into a village and stumbled upon a small shack by the roadside. The shack belonged to an old woman who stayed there all by herself and sold only two things: chai and corn bhajis.

He still remembered the first bite like it was yesterday. He had instinctively closed his eyes, shut everything else out and concentrated only on the sensations on his tongue and in his nose. The bhajis were steaming hot, yet he could taste every ingredient. They were like fireworks in his mouth. He could taste a whole spectrum, an entire palette of flavours. And now that Kavya was going with him, he felt it was going to be perfect.

He sang with happiness out of the love he had for Kavya.

Whenever you rise, it's dawn,
Whenever you sleep, it's dusk.
My day ends and begins with you, love.

You're my light, my sunshine,
the sun rises and sets with you.

He got up and started walking towards her.

He gave Kavya a slight push against the wall and put his hand lovingly on her cheek, looking straight into her eyes.

'You're comfort. You're warmth. You're everything, Kavvu.'

She smiled giddily.

With his right hand, he held her by the waist and pulled her closer. With his left hand he caught hold of her wild curls and tilted her head back, lifting her chin. Her breath reminded him of bubble gum. He leaned in and kissed her passionately. She wrapped her arms around him and kissed him back. After a while he moved back, but didn't let go. Then he softly gave her a peck on the cheek. 'You have ninety seconds to get ready. Hurry up!'

Kavya laughed. She tried to tempt Dhruv, but he pushed her to leave. There was a smile on her face as she went to get dressed.

Watching her, Dhruv realized that it was the best feeling in the world to wake up to such a genuine, passionate and lovely girl each day. And now a round of hot bhajis with a glass of chai would make his day perfect!

2

'You called the cab here?' Kavya looked around the basement of their apartment complex. She couldn't remember the last time she'd risen before the sun; it was still dark outside.

She rubbed her eyes and yawned as she dragged her feet across the parking lot. She was starting to feel sleepy again. Though she tried her best not to show it, because she didn't want to dampen Dhruv's excitement, she had one of those expressive faces that could never conceal what she was feeling.

'Nope, no cab today.' Dhruv put his hand inside his pocket and jangled what seemed to Kavya like loose change. Kavya thought this was his way of telling her that he was too broke to call for a cab.

She panicked for a moment, then took a deep breath and spoke calmly. 'Please let's not take a bus or train. It's Sunday morning, Momo, the last day before I return to that dreadful office. I am too tired, please let's just go back to sleep. I have no energy for this.'

Dhruv smiled and pulled out a set of car keys from his pocket, beaming as he lifted them high enough for Kavya to see.

'You bought a car?' Kavya was baffled and her brain was working really slowly. Her system needed more time to boot.

'Obviously! How else will we go to eat bhajis? We can't take the train or the bus, no?' He had a twinkle in his eyes.

'Really?'

Kavya didn't find it difficult to believe that Dhruv could have bought a car just for this one-day trip.

'Don't be silly! It's Akash's brother's car.'

Now that was a good idea. Kavya relaxed.

'I borrowed it for a day so that we could comfortably go and eat bhajis. It'll be a nice drive.'

Once in the car, Kavya realized what a nice idea it was.

'Yay! This means I can sleep!' She pushed her seat all the way back.

'Seriously?' Despair was evident in Dhruv's voice.

Then, in an exaggerated tone of disbelief, he added, 'Don't you know it's the duty of the person in the passenger seat to be the DJ so that the driver does not fall asleep?' He then held her by the shoulders and shook her dramatically.

'Do you want to get both of us killed? That too over bhajis?'

Kavya made a face as she reluctantly pulled her chair back up.

Little did she know that she'd soon be glad that they took off on this adventure. Even though she didn't know it then, it was going to change her life . . . forever!

* * *

'Oh my God, Dhruv! Just look at the stars!' Kavya squealed with delight as she pointed towards the sky. The sky was getting clearer as they drove away from the heart of the city and into the suburbs.

It wasn't morning yet—the sun hadn't risen—but there was a dim glow in the sky. Kavya rested her hand on Dhruv's as he held the gear stick. They looked at each other for a flash and smiled. They were happy to be doing this.

Dhruv began by turning the music down and then switching it off. A beautiful silence engulfed them as they looked around eagerly. The city looked so different waking up from its slumber. The birds were just stirring, an occasional dog crossed their path, and the newspaper vendors were just getting started.

As they drove across the city towards its borders, the buildings kept getting smaller and further apart and the trees kept getting bigger. Once they were out of the city, all that was visible was dense, abundant greenery and a rain-swept road rising and falling before them. The windows were rolled down, and the morning chill gave them a slight shiver. The fresh air whipping across their faces and filling up their lungs felt reinvigorating and rejuvenating—absolutely worth all the effort.

The thing about living in a city is that you start believing it to be the world. You don't get time to escape from it, and you forget that a whole world exists outside it. Accustomed to living in small, loud, sweaty confines, you forget the cool breeze, the trees, the stars and everything that is soothing about nature.

Dhruv and Kavya made the most of the drive. They even stopped on a small bridge to take selfies and chat. There was not a single car or person in sight, it was just the trees. The sight was so mesmerizing that they had to step out of the car. They held hands and watched the river flow under them.

That was when Kavya broke the silence with the sweetest sound Dhruv had ever heard—the sound of her singing. She rarely sang in front of anyone and had sung to Dhruv only a few times. But when she did, she sounded like an angel. She was in complete harmony with the gushing river, the chirping birds and the swaying trees—as if they were all part of an orchestra that composed the sweetest of symphonies.

Dhruv listened intently, shutting his eyes so that he could concentrate on her voice. When she finished singing, the only reaction he offered was a slight smile, knowing from experience that praise or applause would only set her off, make her feel awkward and reluctant to sing in front of him.

They then took a selfie against the backdrop of the river before heading back into the car.

As they drove, the breeze seemed to gather pace and roll off the meadows on either side of the road.

'I think we're lost.' Dhruv could see nothing but greenery around. He had been driving for long and there was no sight of the bhaji lady yet.

As he desperately looked around, trying to figure out where they were, Kavya asked, 'What exactly are we looking for?'

She was enjoying herself so much that she couldn't understand why Dhruv had become tense.

'Bhajis, Kavya! We're looking for the woman who sells those corn bhajis! That's the reason we left the house, remember?' Dhruv was getting really worked up.

'Calm down! Look, there are two guys up ahead. Let's ask them.'

Dhruv stopped the car a little distance away from the two men who were sitting under a tree. 'Bhaiya, there's an aunty here who sells corn bhajis. Do you know where she sits?'

The two men instantly pointed ahead, she sure was famous here. It was well-deserved fame—Dhruv would attest to that.

'How far ahead?' Dhruv asked.

'Not very far. Just keep going down this road.'

Dhruv was excited again. As they kept driving, things began to look familiar to him. He remembered being there on that blessed day when he had those bhajis for the first time. His stomach started rumbling.

179

As soon as he saw the stall, he knew it was the one. He stopped the car. And then all the excitement, the effort, and the planning came to naught. Under the makeshift tarpaulin, the stall lay cold. The tent fluttered in the breeze. There was no one around.

Kavya saw the look on Dhruv's face and felt sorry for him.

'One second.' She opened the door and started walking towards a small group of people huddled under a tree. Dhruv too got out of the car, locked it and followed her.

Kavya spoke to them in Hindi, but switched to Marathi because that was all that they understood. Dhruv stood alone, unable to understand a word. He waited with bated breath for Kavya to tell him what was going on.

She returned with information.

'She has been gone for four days, and they don't know when she'll be back. Her son had a daughter and she has gone back to her village to see them.'

'Hmm . . . that's something I can't even be angry about.'

'It's okay, Momo. We'll come back for them another day.' She held his hand and tried to comfort him, but it didn't work.

'Let's just go back. I am done for today.'

'Go back? Are you crazy, Dhruv? We've come all the way here and you just want to go back? Just look around you!'

Kavya's sweatshirt and hair fluttered in the breeze. All around them was breathtaking greenery, with a lake in the backdrop. In the distance, the hills stood tall and proud, occasionally disappearing behind passing clouds.

'I don't understand. How can you just want to go back? Are you allergic to pure oxygen or something?' Kavya was flabbergasted.

Dhruv was so fixated on the bhajis that he couldn't understand any of this. He was too busy feeling bad for himself. With arms flailing about, he pretended to take deep breaths, guiding the air up his nostrils with his hands.

'Oxygen! Oxygen! I am parcelling some to take home. Would you also like to pack some for yourself?'

Kavya gave him a pained look and shook her head. She knew it had been a disappointing trip for Dhruv. But it didn't have to be. Hell, this didn't even need to be the end of their trip. They could still try to make the most of it. And who knew, they could even end up enjoying it more than the bhajis.

'Come on, let's just go back home.' Dhruv sounded defeated.

But Kavya didn't want to head back yet. It was a gorgeous day and they were at a pristine location. She was looking around when something caught her eye. She had spotted a small vineyard.

'Hey, is that a vineyard?' The excitement in her voice was palpable.

Dhruv turned his gaze to where she was pointing.

'Yes, so?'

'So? What do you mean "so"? Let's go!'

She caught Dhruv's hand and pulled him towards the vineyard.

Dhruv just wanted to go home. But seeing Kavya's enthusiasm, he couldn't refuse.

Dragging his feet, he followed her reluctantly. At the edge of the vineyard was a small fence. Kavya stepped over it and waited for Dhruv to join her.

'Kavvu, come on, let's go. We'll get into trouble, I'm telling you. I am sure this qualifies as trespassing.' But Kavya was adamant and way too excited to let anything deter her. Of course, he was not going to let her do this alone no matter how irritated and restless he may be. He jumped across and joined her on the other side of the fence.

They walked through grapevines curled around wooden frames. They could see grapes hanging from the vines.

'Just relax, Momo. This is thrilling!' The excitement in Kavya's voice had doubled.

'I still think we should go back. I sure would be pissed off if I caught some kids breaking into my vineyard.' Dhruv remained reluctant.

'But it's not like we are touching the grapes. Why should we be scared?'

Dhruv gave up trying to reason with her. As Kavya hopped, skipped and frolicked in the vineyard, the beauty of the surroundings was lost on Dhruv. He was unable to get over his disappointment.

'Hey, look!' Kavya pointed to a bunch of grapes. She moved closer, picked one out and bit into it.

'No, don't do that!' Dhruv smacked his forehead. 'What is this, Kavvu? You need to wash them at least. God knows how much pesticide you must have consumed with that one bite.'

But Kavya couldn't care less. She was having an awesome time and was not going to let Dhruv bring her down.

'Ummm . . . interesting . . .' She kept chewing on the grape. Then, looking into the distance, she said, 'I think they make Chardonnay out of these.'

And just like that Kavya was an expert on grapes and wine! Her only qualification—she was standing in a vineyard, tasting a grape.

'Really? If you say so.' Dhruv was disinterested.

'Do you want to try one?'

'No.'

Dhruv began walking ahead, looking into his phone. Kavya picked up pebbles and, with an impish smile, began throwing them at Dhruv. He ignored it for some time but finally lost patience.

'Stop it, Kavvu!'

'Then you stop being on your phone, loser!'

'I'm just checking to see if Sturridge is fit for today's game.'

Even all these miles away from the bustle of the city, in a vast green expanse, Dhruv couldn't help but think about the Liverpool football player—that too in the middle of a vineyard. He couldn't appreciate the beauty around him, while Kavya was thoroughly enjoying it.

'Okay, but at least don't do it here. Look around, take things in, feel the wind, the greenery of this vineyard . . . the smell of the earth. What you're doing is criminal. Such a waste!'

Dhruv, however, was very practical in his approach.

185

'Kavya, you know this place is only two hours from Mumbai, right? We can come here any time of the week. But you are a sloth bear. So, things like these . . .'

'Shut up!' Kavya cut him off playfully. 'It's very difficult to be in my shoes, okay? I love my sleep. You couldn't fathom my love for it even if you wanted to . . .'

'Excuse me, Sir!' someone cut into their conversation. Both Dhruv and Kavya turned to find a man dressed formally in black with an apron on. On his apron was the name of the vineyard.

'Have you come from Mumbai?'

Dhruv realized that they had been caught and wanted to avoid any kind of trouble or conflict. 'I am so sorry . . . we were just . . .'

'Er . . . your group's wine tasting session is about to begin. You can join them at the wine cellar in the basement, Sir.'

This was an interesting turn of events, and Kavya's interest was immediately piqued.

'We're not with the group. But how much is it for?'

'It's for just Rs 250.'

'That's it? Let's go!'

With this, Kavya started marching towards the man without even consulting Dhruv. She knew he'd complain initially, but would ultimately enjoy himself and be thankful that he'd done it—just like it had happened at Shifa's party.

Dhruv looked at her smile and the skip in her step. He knew she really wanted to do this. As he followed her to the cellar, he started feeling better. The disappointment was wearing off. Maybe, just maybe, it wasn't as bad a day as he'd made it out to be.

3

'Wine tasting is all about the three S's: smell, swirl and sip.'

This was the same guy Dhruv and Kavya had met in the vineyard.

They were in the cellar with more than eighty people who had come all the way to learn about wine-making and tasting. Dhruv had lightened up—the thought of alcohol had put him in a surprisingly good mood! Both of them stood in the centre of the room, ready to drink and have a great time. But they weren't very serious about the tasting. For them, it was just an interesting thing to do.

'Hi! My name is Suresh, and I'll be your guide in the art of wine tasting today. For the first step, please put your nose to the glass and try smelling the wine.'

Dhruv and Kavya looked awkwardly at each other. They didn't know if they were actually up for this. They just wanted to get to the part where you drink the wine.

'Go on,' Suresh urged. It smelt like any other wine. Dhruv was in an exceptionally playful mood by now. He held Kavya's glass against her nose and did not let go till she smacked him on the back of his head.

Meanwhile, Suresh continued . . .

'Now, this particular wine is called the rosé. Its salmon-pink colour is because of the pressure we put on the seed, the juice and the skin . . .'

Everyone, except Kavya and Dhruv, was extremely serious about the wine tasting and hung on to each of Suresh's words.

'In the second step, swirl. Move your glass like this.' Suresh demonstrated by rotating his glass, ensuring it was parallel to the ground at all times. Dhruv, however, got too enthusiastic about the swirling and managed to disturb the elderly gentleman in front of him. He was rewarded with a dirty look. Kavya and Dhruv sniggered, least bothered about what was being said . . .

'By swirling the wine, we're giving it more oxygen to open up. Now, smell it again. You might notice some difference; it starts to smell a bit different.'

Both of them put their noses into their glasses—it smelt the same to them. But they pretended like they noticed a difference.

'It smells sweeter!' someone declared.

'Yes, it does, Sir.'

'It surely does!' Kavya shouted.

Dhruv nudged her, asking her to keep it down. The wine seemed to be hitting her already.

'In the third step—the sip—take a sip and then gargle with it. In doing so, we provide the wine with some more oxygen.'

Kavya didn't care about gargling or sipping, she downed the whole glass. Dhruv showed a little more restraint. He emptied the glass in his mouth and began gargling noisily. The elderly gentleman once again turned to scowl at them. Dhruv came really close to Kavya's face and started gargling in her ear.

'I wish I could use wine as mouthwash every day,' Kavya said. Dhruv found this so funny that he laughed and spilled the wine on the scowling gentleman's shirt.

'What is this? This is no way to behave! Be serious!'

Suresh tried to calm him down.

'No problem, Sir. I will get you napkins.' He tried to pacify the gentleman while glancing at Kavya and Dhruv with a mixed expression on his face.

Dhruv apologized, but Kavya continued to snigger.

With the gentleman now placated, Suresh continued. 'Wine tasting is an art to be savoured drop by drop, sip by sip, bit by bit . . .'

Suresh then took the group around the cellar and the brewery, showing them the process of making a good bottle of wine. All this while, there were trays of wine samples going around. By the time they were done with the tour, Kavya had had several glasses.

When the tour finally ended, Suresh bid them goodbye. But even then, Kavya kept finding more samples and gulping them down. Finally, one of the servers came up to them, asked them to move on and escorted them to the restaurant.

Once they were there, Kavya went up to the bar, grabbed a bottle of wine and drank straight from it. Dhruv was a little taken aback, but then he simply shrugged and laughed. Who was he to stop her from having a good time on a hard-earned weekend?

'Kavvu, I'll stop drinking now and sober up. I need to drive back. You can continue.'

And continue she did, swigging the wine through their lavish brunch. Just as they finished eating, Kavya looked at Dhruv. 'I can't believe we came here to have bloody bhajis!'

Both of them burst out laughing. It really was strange how they had come to do one thing and ended up doing something totally different!

There was silence for a while as both of them looked through a huge window that overlooked the vineyard. Dhruv got up and asked Kavya, 'Are you done? Let's go for a walk? The vineyard looks gorgeous right now.'

'Wait a second! You're enjoying this now? Didn't you want to just go home? You always make a big fuss about new experiences and then end up enjoying yourself once you are actually there.'

She wasn't complaining, just making an observation. She loved him exactly the way he was.

'*Haan*, haan. Sorry, Baba. I don't know, but it's very difficult for me to get over disappointment so quickly and look at the bright side. Thank you for being you, Kavvu. I would not have had half the experiences that I have if it wasn't for you.'

'Okay, okay. There's no reason to get so emotional, Momo . . .' Kavya had started slurring and swaying a little.

'Race you till the vineyard!' She began running towards the exit.

'Be careful, don't fall down the stairs!' Dhruv ran after her.

Kavya stopped right there, not because she paid heed to Dhruv's advice but because she had forgotten the bottle of wine at the table. She ran back, picked it up and once again rushed towards the door.

Both of them reached the vineyard almost at the same time, laughing. They were once again reminded that as long as they were together, they would always have a good time.

* * *

Dhruv and Kavya walked together in silence, going over the day so far in their minds. Kavya took a huge swig from the bottle. That morning had taught her something, and she wanted to share it with Dhruv.

'Dhruv, I have been thinking . . . Should I quit my job?'

'What!'

'It's just that I have not been enjoying it for a while now.' They were now walking between the vines. Kavya was still holding the bottle.

Dhruv gave her a knowing smile. 'I know, I could see that. I could see your frustration building.'

'Then why did you not say anything?'

'Because I wanted you to say it yourself, which you did! So it's all good. In consumer studies, this theory is known as "revealed preferences". It basically means that your actions reveal what you want. How cool is that?'

'I guess it is . . .' Kavya was deep in thought. 'But it's so scary, no? What if I quit my job and never figure out what I want to do?'

Dhruv took the bottle from Kavya for a gulp.

'Okay, let's assume you quit your job. And let's say there is a 50 per cent chance that when you quit . . .'

'Stop right there, Dhruv. Please for once don't talk in terms of probability. Talk simply, talk like a normal person.'

Dhruv understood. Not everything could be broken down into statistics and probability. And even if it could, it wasn't necessarily the best way to explain everything.

'Let me put it simply then. If you quit your job to figure out what you want to do, then it is not a waste of time. Simple.'

Kavya gave him a wry look that indicated he wasn't taking her seriously. Dhruv thought for a moment and looked at Kavya.

'Pros and cons—let's do pros and cons and take a call.'

They walked out of the vineyard and found a nice patch of grass that faced the lake and the hills.

'Okay, pros first or cons?'

Kavya wanted to save the best for the last, so she went with cons.

Dhruv placed the bottle of wine down and collected a few pebbles. The idea was that for every pro, he'd place a stone to the right of the bottle, and for a con to the left. He then began listing the cons.

'So, you won't be earning anything.' He placed a pebble to the left of the bottle. 'You may run out of savings. Your parents may not understand your decision at first. Everybody around you will be getting richer, and that's bound to make you jealous.'

Kavya was getting sadder by the minute.

'Some lifestyle changes will have to be made. Even though I'm here to support you, you know you'll have to cut back on some things. It may not look good on your CV, and it could be a while before you find another job. Honestly, there is a possibility that you could just be more confused after this . . .'

This was more than what Kavya could handle.

'No, no more. That's enough. Pros now.' They hadn't started with the pros yet and the pebbles on the left side were filling her with dread.

'Hmm . . . pros . . . pros . . .' Dhruv thought hard, but for the longest time he could not come up with anything.

'What the hell!' Kavya was getting really disheartened.

'Wait a second, it takes time, Kavya . . . I am thinking.'

Finally, Dhruv spoke. 'Yes! The break may help you understand whether you want to continue working in sales or not. You might want to explore a completely different career path.'

Kavya felt a little better.

'You can become one of those dog babysitters!'

'Dog-sitter, you mean?' A smile lit up Kavya's face. 'Yes, that is a pretty cool job. And it's a thing these days.'

Dhruv was on a roll. 'All right! So you could travel, read more, paint more, draw more. Ummm . . . you can just explore yourself. Just do new things—basically, grow!' he said with his arms spread wide.

'Stop. You are just repeating yourself now.' Kavya smiled at his attempts to come up with more pros.

'You figured it out. Anyway, there are more cons than pros.'

'Yeah. But I like the pros more than the cons, no matter how few they are. I'm seriously going to think about it.' There was relief and sombreness on her face.

Dhruv knew he had to lighten the mood as the conversation was getting too intense.

'So, it's true, huh? When you come to a good, clean place like this, with pure oxygen, it does cleanse your mind. Helps you get more clarity. By the way, I'm taking full credit for this.' He leaned into Kavya, who was smiling widely.

'Really? You wanted to go back hours ago, the moment you saw that the bhaji stall was shut. I spotted this place, I decided to take the tour . . .'

'Yes, but we came here because of me, because of my quest for bhajis. So, you see, it all comes down to me.'

Kavya had turned philosophical again.

'It's not about the place anyway. I was fine till you posted that video on Facebook.'

'Which one . . .'

'The Bangalore girl.'

'Oh, the poem?'

'Yes, the one who talks about what it feels like to be an introvert . . .'

'Yes, I remember that one. What about it?'

Kavya tore a few blades of grass.

'It's not like I'm an introvert or anything. It's just that I really liked the way she expressed herself, you know? I wonder if I have ever expressed myself so clearly.'

'You must have.' Dhruv was looking at her intently.

'I don't know . . . Maybe I did when I was a kid. But it stopped once I grew up. I used to concentrate so hard when I would paint. I used to be such an active kid in school—debate clubs, cultural events, sports . . . I used to be a part of everything. I was always at the top of my game, all the freaking time! I really enjoyed being busy and tired.'

She stopped for a while, looked around, took a deep breath and carried on.

'You know, I thought that when I grew up, I'd be something, that I'd do something really kick-ass. I loved to surprise myself. That hasn't happened in a long time now. I think I have just become . . .'

'Lazy?'

'No!' Kavya looked offended. 'Not lazy.'

Dhruv looked at her questioningly. She looked back at him.

'Okay, fine. Lazy.'

Dhruv smiled.

Kavya looked into the distance. 'I hate that word. I have become lazy not just physically but also mentally.'

She continued hesitantly. 'Don't take this the wrong way, but . . .'

Dhruv urged her to go on.

'Most of the things that we do . . . are the things that you want to do. And I love doing them because I love spending time with you. I always have a ball when I am with you. But, honestly, it takes a lot more out of me than you to travel two hours on a Sunday to just have some bhajis or cutlets . . .'

Dhruv was a bit stumped. 'So, wait. You didn't come here for the bhajis?'

'Of course not. I came here for us. We haven't got out of the city for the longest time. I thought we could do with some time together.'

This softened Dhruv.

'And there's another reason, but I'll tell you about that later.'

'Well, okay, at least you are thinking about these things. You just have to figure out some of them and you'll be fine. This is good. This is a step in the right direction.'

'You're sounding very formal, you know?'

'Yeah, that's because I'm serious.' Both of them stared into the distance, at the lake and the hills. There was silence for a few moments before Kavya spoke up.

'You didn't feel bad about what I said, right?'

'Are you crazy? Not at all. You're expressing yourself so well, opening up to me so freely, why would I feel bad? This is nice. This is really nice. Every time we go out, we have fun. We should do this more often.'

'I know . . . It's funny how so many girls my age are busy getting married and travelling, some are doing so well professionally. And here I am, trying to quit my job and start something completely new. And I don't even know what.'

'You're just trying to figure out a way to make everyday life more fun and fulfilling. Not many people think like that, Kavya Kulkarni. So this is a good thing. Chill!'

'It's true. And you know, the dog-sitter job is actually a good idea.'

Kavya took a deep breath, looked at Dhruv's soothing, knowing smile and felt better.

'Great! Now say, "Thank you, Kundan!"'

She giggled and looked at him. 'Thank you, Dhruv.'

'Wow, manners! Where did that come from?' Dhruv laughed and defused the situation.

'That's because I am feeling really light right now!'

With this, Kavya stretched out on the vast mattress of grass. Dhruv lay down beside her. The grass was cold, soft and a little moist because of the dew—it felt so good.

'I don't want to go back to Mumbai. Like, seriously,' he said with a smile. Kavya smiled too, taking in the statement that was totally unlike Dhruv.

She decided it was time he knew.

'I didn't come here for the bhajis, silly! I came here because . . .' Kavya pointed to her colourful, round earrings.

Dhruv didn't get the hint. 'Nice, they look pretty.'

'You don't remember, do you?'

'Remember what?'

'That exactly two years ago, we met for the first time, in that movie hall.'

'No, I don't think it is today. It's tomorrow. Let me check, I have the tickets in my wallet.'

'Let's do this.' Kavya seemed to be absolutely sure.

He pulled out his wallet from his pocket and took out a neatly folded piece of paper. He opened it and stared at the date—he'd got it wrong. It was indeed the day on which they had first met two years ago! He sheepishly put the tickets back, then turned to Kavya and grinned.

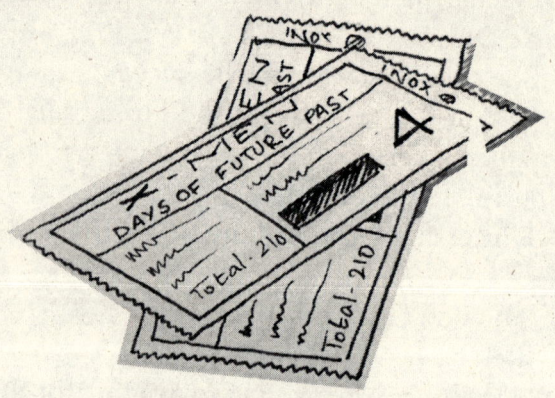

They remembered how they had noticed each other in the movie hall, both of them watching the film alone. Later that evening they had shared an autorickshaw and Kavya had come to his house. They'd chatted nineteen to the dozen, losing track of time. It wasn't long before they moved in together. Those were happy memories.

'Love you,' Kavya said softly.

'I love you too.' Dhruv put his arm under her head. He gave her a peck on the cheek and both of them held each other, looking at the sky. Kavya fell asleep—she felt so carefree, safe and warm in his arms. Dhruv didn't move lest he woke her up. He loved being there with Kavya. It felt like they were meant to be there in that moment, on that day.

They lay there till the sun had nearly descended and it had started getting dark.

* * *

Dhruv came out of the shower and went to the kitchen to turn off the pot of coffee he had set to brew. Kavya had already had a shower and was busy doing something. They had returned home exhausted but feeling great. It was time for bed.

As he entered the room, Dhruv saw Kavya putting up a picture on the wall behind them—

the one that was full of Kavya's drawings, the one that had sketches of their outings, even the one at the movie hall!

Dhruv came closer to see what it was and was pleasantly surprised. It was a sketch of him and Kavya walking hand-in-hand, between rows and rows of vines. For added detail, Kavya had even sketched a bottle of wine in one hand. On the bottom right corner was the date and her signature.

'Wow, this is so nice! When did you make it?'
'When you were taking a bath.'

Soon after, they snuggled up in bed with coffee and their books. It had been a perfect date, a perfect anniversary. Nothing loud, over-the-top, or special—just everyday stuff.

They knew that there was nowhere else they would rather be, nothing else they would rather do.

Because what is life and love, if not for the little things?